CONFLICT OF INTEREST

A LAKE CHELAN NOVEL, BOOK 7

SHIRLEY PENICK

CONFLICT OF INTEREST

Copyright 2019 by Shirley Penick

All rights reserved. No part of this work may be reproduced in any fashion without the express written consent of the copyright holder.

CONFLICT OF INTEREST is a work of fiction. All characters and events portrayed herein are fictitious and are not based on any real persons living or dead.

Photography by Jean Woodfin

Cover Models: Katy McCain and Dan Rengering

Contact me:

www.shirleypenick.com

www.facebook.com/ShirleyPenickAuthor

To sign up for Shirley's New Release Newsletter, send email to shirleypenick@outlook.com, subject newsletter.

To my boss, Jasmine, because you have been very supportive of my writing from day one and because you wanted me to put you in a book.
Jacqueline certainly has your work ethic, but she is a fictional character.
Betsy on the other hand is not and I want to thank Judia Burns Jackson for loaning us Betsy, who is, after-all, the star of the story.

CHAPTER ONE

Lake Chelan

Jacqueline Hurst hit the send button on her phone with hope in her exhausted heart, that this idea would work. "Sandy, hi it's Jacqueline."

Sandy's cheery voice came over the line. "Jacqueline, to what do I owe the pleasure of this call? I saw our contract was finalized, so I know you're not calling to fire me."

"No, not calling to fire you, but I need a break after that court case against the saboteurs. You would think we were the ones that broke laws by the attitudes I came across. Why we had to jump through all those hoops to prove it was sabotage against our company, I will never know. That we had to prove that we didn't deliberately hire that *supposed* intern to work for us. We're a video game company, one of our flagship games—for children—had very edgy porn hidden in it. Why they would even consider we might do that to ourselves is beyond me. Their reasoning was ridiculous."

"I know boss, I'm so sorry you had to take point on this."

"Okay, I know, preaching to the choir. Just be glad you didn't have to face them. It is my job as the business lead of the game team to do it. I just hope it never, ever, happens again."

She sighed and tried to let her frustration go. They had finally won the case. She needed to move on. She drew in a deep breath and tried to sound cheerful. "Anyway, I was hoping I could take you up on your offer to stay at your mom's Bed and Breakfast."

"Of course, how soon were you thinking?"

Jacqueline looked around her home. She loved it, with its mid-century modern theme, and her Lane Acclaim vintage tables. But right now, she wanted to be far, far away from it. She wanted nothing to remind her of the last eight months of legalese torture. "Yesterday? For a week or even two."

"Sorry, I can't do time travel yet. Let me look at what's available. I'm so glad I finally talked Mom into letting me put everything online."

Jacqueline prayed there was a vacancy, she needed a break. Far away from Seattle. Lake Chelan wasn't a great distance, only a few hours' drive over the mountains to eastern Washington, but Sandy's hometown was remote enough to unplug.

"You're in luck we've got an opening starting today for two weeks, want me to pencil you in?"

"Not pencil, use a sharpie, thick and bold, that no one can erase."

Sandy laughed. "Done, you'll have to take the ferry or seaplane to get here. Are you planning to drive over or take a flight?"

"Hmm, I hadn't thought about flying. I was contemplating driving Betsy over."

"You could be here tonight if you can book a flight, otherwise you'll have to catch the ferry in the morning at eight thirty and leave Betsy in Chelan. I don't think you'll want to leave your classic car in some parking lot for two weeks. Or, no wait, you could bring her along if you booked passage on the barge, for you and her. Let me look... it is running tomorrow. The barge runs a little later in the day, so you wouldn't have to be in Chelan until ten. You could bring Betsy along. She would probably love the cruise through the mountains."

"She would, but getting there fast might be nice, too. I'll do some investigation and text you to let you know for sure."

"Sounds good, it will be fun to have you visit for a while. And it will definitely be relaxing. Maybe even boring." Sandy laughed.

"Just what the doctor ordered. See you soon."

As she hung up, Jacqueline imagined taking Betsy for a leisurely journey through the mountains and into Chelan. It had been a while since she'd taken the '56 Chevy Bel Air on a trip that far, but she knew the older car would hold up, she made sure Betsy was well taken care of and always in top operating form. Betsy was her one indulgence. The car had never let her down, unlike humans. She was her one true love, far superior to *some* man.

Those lawyers had left a sour taste in her mouth, even *their* lawyer had been a first-class jerk. Clearly, he was of the old school where women were of no consequence in business. It had severely ticked her off.

No, she wasn't going to think about him, she refused to allow her thoughts to be invaded by the nasty, misogynistic, creep.

She was only going to envision driving her car through the mountains into Chelan. Even if she didn't need to be there until ten, she would have to get up early. It was about a four-hour drive. But with the prospect of a two-week vacation on the horizon she wouldn't mind getting up and being on the road before six.

Obviously, her mind was made up. She brought up the

barge's home page and booked a slot. Then she texted Sandy.

Jacqueline: I'm driving and will arrive on the barge. Yay!
Sandy: I'll have a glass of iced tea ready with your name on it.
Sandy: Or maybe a margarita would be better.
Jacqueline: LOL
Sandy: I'll have both and you can pick.
Jacqueline: Awesome. I can't wait.
Sandy: See you soon!
Jacqueline: Yay!!!!!

Jacqueline hurried to her room to pack; this was going to be glorious.

~

The cool air from the air-conditioning rushed over David Williams's skin as he sauntered into the dim lighting of Greg's bar. He stopped right inside the door to let his eyes adjust from the bright sunlight outside.

When he could see again, he raised one hand to the man who had been his nemesis from the time he was about eight, until a few years ago when Greg Jones had left his father's law firm, and had returned to his home town to run this bar.

David had thought Greg was a fool back then, but in hindsight, he realized Greg had been the wise one, to escape the machinations of David's father. After a lot of counseling and many months, David had recognized that Greg had never been the problem, it had been his father pitting him against Greg that had caused all the issues.

From their first pee-wee baseball team right on through college and their internships at the law firm, David's father had always degraded his own son and lauded Greg. It had been a really poor attempt to make David try harder. Instead, it had caused enmity with a man that could have, and probably should have, been his best friend.

Greg nodded in his direction. "To what do we owe the pleasure of your appearance in our town and my bar especially?"

David raised his hand and ticked off the reasons as he spoke. "One, getting the hell out of Seattle. Two, getting the hell out of the office. Three, getting away from my father. Four, coming to see Mom. Five, trying to use up some vacation time. Six, checking on everyone's favorite pyromaniac."

Greg said, "Former pyromaniac. You'll be pleased to hear he's totally reformed, loving his job creating glass art, an excellent asset to the fire department, and a mighty fine bass guitarist in the church's worship band. You did a good thing getting him probation and allowing him to work with Nolan rather than going to jail."

David accepted Greg's praise with the stoicism that had been drilled into him by his father. Never show another man your hand, and be as ruthless as possible, was his father's motto. "Good to know."

"So, that explains your visit to Chelan. What brings you into my bar? I don't recall you *ever* darkening my door." Greg raised an eyebrow at him in question.

"You just answered part of it, checking up on Kent. But I also decided a beer sounded good and maybe a snack. You sell some kind of food, don't you?" David pointed to the draft he wanted as he spoke.

"Anything that can be fried," Greg said, already pulling the beer.

"Fish and chips?"

Greg nodded. "Frozen, not fresh."

"Fine with me," David said as Greg slid the beer in front of him.

"Be right back."

As Greg walked away, David thought about what he really wanted to do in Greg's bar, and that was to hopefully reconcile with the man. His father had been a cruel bastard, to both of them, and while David couldn't exactly make amends for that behavior, he hoped that he and Greg could at least be... if not friends, at least not enemies, frenemies maybe.

When Greg came back with his order and set the condiments on the bar in front of him David decided he'd at least start the conversation he wanted to have with Greg. It would probably take a while to get it all out on the table, so taking the first step would be good.

He picked up the ketchup and squirted it onto the plate next to the fries. "I decided on my way here that you were the wiser of the two of us."

Surprise flashed in Greg's eyes, but he quickly hid it. "How so?"

"You got out from under my father's thumb."

"Your father's a dick," Greg said conversationally, no ire in his voice at all.

David snorted. "After many years of counseling, I've finally figured that out."

"However, I didn't leave the firm to get out from under his thumb, that was just a nice by-product. I left because I felt what the firm did was unethical."

David was only slightly surprised by that. "It can be."

"I went into the law to make things right, better. Those internships only shed the light on the fact that lawyers—or at least the lawyers in your father's firm—either got the criminals off with a slap on the wrist, or screwed over the little guys, so the big corporations didn't have to pay out."

"That does happen. I don't deny it."

Greg folded his arms over his chest. "I couldn't do that, day in and day out."

David chuckled. "No, I can see that, you've always had a bit of a hero complex."

Narrowed eyes told him Greg was about to take offense,

which was totally not what he was going for. He held up his hand in a stop sign way.

"Not in a bad way, Jones." He ticked off the fingers of his hand as he recounted all that Greg did for the town. "You're a saver, you're the fire chief, you are always helping out at the old folks' center. Hell, you raised enough money on that fundraiser to keep the people of this town in emergency flights to Chelan for years." He pointed at the man. "You don't just talk about helping people or about what's right or wrong, you put your money where your mouth is. Or if not your money, your back and sweat equity."

Greg relaxed and shrugged. "I had help with all those things. I'm not the Lone Ranger."

"Nobody said you needed to be. But it would go against the grain to do just the opposite of those things, in a legal setting, that could ruin lives."

"Yeah, that's why I left."

"And you, lucky bastard, you got away from the asshole who was always pitting us against each other. I envy you not having to deal with him."

"Your father?"

David sneered. "Good old dad."

"What do you mean by pitted us against one another?"

David's chuckle was bitter, thinking about all the ways his father had held Greg's abilities over his head. David's self-esteem had plummeted with each word uttered by the man he wanted to be proud of him. He'd held a grudge against Greg, and none of it had been Greg's fault. "The reason we were at loggerheads so much of our lives is because my dear father always held you up as the shining example of what I should be striving for."

"Are you shitting me?"

"I wish I was." He counted on his fingers again. "Nope, you were a better pitcher on the baseball team. You were a better runner. You were a better student in college. You were a better intern. You would make a better lawyer."

Greg's mouth was hanging open in shock. "I had no idea. So that's why you were always hostile, always trying to put me down or do better."

"Yeah, and I'm not proud of that. Of course, I didn't really know it at the time. I wasn't joking about therapy. My counselor is the one that helped me to see, recognize, and understand exactly what my father had accomplished. He might have even done it deliberately with the purpose to make me as much of an asshole as he is."

Greg shook his head. "Well, that does explain a lot, doesn't it? I take it he didn't succeed in his goals."

"No, thank God my mother talked me into getting counseling. I was on the road to ruin. Drinking too much, driving too fast, fucking every female I could. It wasn't pretty."

Greg shook his head. "Self-destruction is never attractive."

"No, it's not." David was surprised that Greg had figured that out so quickly. He'd said far more than he'd intended, but it was cleansing, somehow. He took up his fish, dunked it into the tartar sauce and filled his mouth.

Greg looked him in the eye. "Thanks for telling me, man. And your father just moved from dick to… I don't even know what, fucker isn't strong enough." Then he started wiping down the spotless bar, giving David the space to eat in peace.

And peace was exactly what he felt, the enmity between the two of them had always weighed on him. David couldn't have asked for this conversation to go any better than it had. When he left the bar there was a spring in his step, that hadn't been there before. Damn, it was good to be back home.

CHAPTER TWO

Lake Chelan

David sat down to dinner with his mother. She'd fussed and made all his favorites. "It looks delicious, Mom. But I would have been more than happy to take you out to Amber's place."

"I know, Davey. We can do that later. I was too excited that you were coming not to cook a few of your favorites."

David smiled at his mom and was glad he'd gone to Greg's early enough that he was hungry for dinner. "I always have loved your cooking, Mom. I've missed it living in Seattle."

A sadness crossed his mother's eyes and she tapped her fork on her plate. "I've missed you too, Davey. Now eat up so this all doesn't get cold."

"Yes, ma'am." He loaded his plate with his mother's meatloaf and creamy mashed potatoes. Steamed veggies with cheddar cheese sprinkled on top and his favorite fruit salad with mandarin orange slices.

He'd taken his first bite of meatloaf and potatoes when his mom asked, "You don't mind staying at Mayor, um former Mayor Carol's B&B, do you? I'm sorry I turned your room into a sewing room."

Is that what was bothering her? He swallowed the deliciousness and said, "No, Mom, I don't mind at all. You should use that room. It's silly to have it sitting empty when it can be utilized. The B&B is very comfortable, and I've got a nice room. Ms. Anderson said she was glad to have me."

"Carol has always been a very sweet lady. It's still hard not to see her leading the city. This is one of only a few times we haven't had an Anderson at the helm."

David knew the town's history as well as anyone. The Anderson's had been one of the founding families. They'd helped establish law and order during at a time where there'd been little civilization. The placer miners, Chinese, and Wenatchee Native Americans had all vied for their place on the lake.

When the Andersons and a few others had founded the city of Chedwick, the others had happily given the job of organization to Jeb Anderson. From that time on, nearly every mayor had been an Anderson. The fact that Carol Anderson—who'd married into the name—and stepped down from being the mayor after almost twenty years, had changed the face of things a few years ago, by pulling the citizens together to save their town, and made the change of leadership hard on many.

"Maybe someday you can talk Sandy into being the mayor. She's an Anderson by birth. Terry doesn't quite have the constitution for being mayor and no one knows what Janet will be like, now that she's out from under the influence of her brutal husband." David might live in the city, but he kept his ears open to the goings-on in what he considered his hometown, regardless of how his father had tried to change that opinion.

His mother nodded. "That would be good, and Greg is

such a decent man, having the two of them would be spectacular."

David had started to bristle at the mention of Greg, before he reminded himself that his mother had never been the one to hold comparisons between the two. Greg was not the problem and all blame lay at his father's feet. And in fact, he agreed that Sandy and Greg would make an excellent team at the helm of their small town. So, he nodded and shoveled more food into his mouth.

~

Jacqueline was so darn excited to get out of town and away from her job for two whole weeks, she was worried she wouldn't be able to sleep, and that would not do. She had to get up early to get Betsy on the road headed toward Lake Chelan.

She'd spent the evening dragging out all the summer clothes she never wore to work. Sundresses, shorts, tank tops, and even swimsuits. Two swimsuits! She had flipflops and strappy sandals and tennis shoes. Oh, it was going to be a glorious two weeks.

No business attire, no practical pumps, and no laptop. She'd left it firmly shut on her desk. She'd considered locking it in the desk drawer, so it wouldn't tempt her to take it along, but then she'd realized she didn't want it. This was not a working vacation, this was a pure unadulterated, no holds barred break.

She tried to think back to the last time she'd taken a vacation and could honestly not remember ever taking one, once she'd received her master's degree in business, and gotten her first job, she'd worked, nonstop. When she'd realized that, it had firmly cemented her decision to leave the computer at home. She was thirty-six and she'd never had an adult vacation, and that was just sad.

Of course, if the company really needed something, they could call her cell and if they managed to convince her she absolutely had to get online, she could use Sandy's machine. But she honestly couldn't find one single thing they could even ask about. The budget for the next fiscal year was set and approved. The contracts were signed, the purchase orders opened and approved.

The court case was finished. The hacker and the company that had hired him had been found guilty. Only the sentencing remained, and she wasn't needed for that. She'd delegated her various roles to her administrative staff, and her desk and email was cleared. So, there was not one single thing that anyone should need her for.

She laid in the dark as she ticked off everything in her mind and found nothing lurking. With a contented sigh, she closed her eyes and let herself drift, on the visions of sitting by the lake with her feet in the water.

CHAPTER THREE

The drive over the mountains was beautiful and relaxing. Not one thing had gone wrong or even been a challenge. Leaving so early in the morning with the sun just starting to rise, there had been no traffic in the city or metro area. Jacqueline had decided to take highway two rather than the interstate. It was a prettier route and avoided all the semis that used the main highway.

She'd stopped into a quaint coffeeshop and bakery in Leavenworth for a quick breakfast, taking a large cup of coffee with her for the rest of the drive into Chelan. When she'd arrived at the ferry dock at nine-fifteen and was all checked in by nine-twenty, the lady at the check-in desk had suggested she might want to take a stroll, since they didn't need her back until nine-forty-five.

Jacqueline took them up on their suggestion and bought some touristy stuff. One was a baseball cap that said 'Lake hair, don't care' on it. She'd never even owned a baseball cap, so she found it quite appropriate. In the little bookstore, she bought two novels. Two! One modern-day thriller and one historical romance. She was giddy with the idea of reading *two* novels.

Betsy was loaded on the barge with a great deal of admiration by the crew. There wasn't any real seating on the barge and she didn't want to stay in Betsy, she spied a spot on the side that was out of the way and had a railing she could hold and headed for that spot. That way she could see the lake as they traversed it. The town Sandy lived in was halfway up the fifty-mile long lake, in an area so remote that it took a boat or a four-wheel drive to get there, or a seaplane. Which made it exactly perfect for her getaway.

It was a gorgeous day with a sky so blue it almost hurt to look at it, a half dozen little puffy clouds only emphasized the blue. The lake was a much deeper darker blue and the mountains in the distance also took on their own shade of dark blue. It was quite a stunning vista. As they moved past the town of Manson, she could see lots of vineyards, some blueberry farms, and even apple orchards.

The barge chugged along moving uplake at a slow but steady pace. Stress slowly purged out of her body with every passing mile. Her stomach settled, her shoulders relaxed, her headache eased. She hadn't even realized how bad the stress had been, hadn't noticed that she hurt all over from the tension.

She was going to spend some time on this trip deciding how to keep stress at bay. Or at the very least find some coping mechanisms for when she couldn't avoid it entirely. Her job wasn't always this stressful. This set of circumstances had been way over the top. The attempted sabotage and corporate espionage was bad enough. Scrambling to find the pornography embedded in their game and the forced delay of the release had given the whole team fits.

But the kicker had been their lawyer, the one whom they had

hired to defend them and prosecute the other company, coming in and treating them like they were the criminals. He'd poo-pooed Sandy's evidence, treated Jacqueline as if she were a moron, and even insinuated that they had deliberately hired the man to make the other company look bad. At first, she'd wondered if he was really working for the other company and had suggested that maybe they needed to hire a different lawyer.

The owner and the head of her division had met with the guy over a round of golf, where the good-old-boy network was in full display. After that, she had finally realized the lawyer's lousy attitude was because they were female. The man was a first-class misogynistic jerk.

Okay, this was old news, and thinking back over it was causing the tension to return. There was no way she was going to let Mr. Henry Williams ruin her vacation.

~

David went by the glass studio, to see in person, how well his former pyromaniac client was doing in his new role, as glass artist and volunteer firefighter. He'd watched Kent for several minutes, so absorbed in the glass that he hadn't even noticed David's presence, which had set his mind to ease. When Kent finally spotted him, the grin that covered the young man's face had erased the remaining questions, and he knew—beyond a shadow of a doubt—he'd done the right thing in getting him probation instead of a jail cell.

Kent carefully tucked away what he was working on and stood, pulling off the thick gloves to join David and enthusiastically pump his hand, not letting go until David had to practically wrench his hand away.

"I take it you're pleased with your situation," David said as he tried to get the blood to flow back into his hand and his arm to stop tingling. The guy had buffed out since he'd last seen him.

Kent laughed and his eyes lit up with joy. "That would be like the understatement of the century. I love it. I've learned so much, both here and on the department. My new shrink is amazing. He's gotten to the root of some of my issues. The guy back in Colorado was great, but he had such a big practice that he didn't have the time to focus."

"But out here in the boonies—"

"Exactly. He's helped me to see that I'm an extreme introvert. I can be friendly and outgoing, but it puts me in a stressful state. So, when I had a people-facing job, I was always on edge, then when something happened that was traumatic, I couldn't handle it and acted out. Now that my job is solitary, I can handle the ups and downs of life. Even the true emergencies we take care of on the fire department."

"I'm really happy to see you're getting the help you need. You've buffed out some."

Kent grinned. "Yeah, from both the fire department and the glass-work. Holding that heavy rod while I sculpt the glass isn't easy without some muscle."

"Makes sense."

"I can't thank you enough for getting me probation rather than having me spend years in jail."

"I'm rewarded by seeing you make something of your life," David said it, and really meant what he said. He felt a huge sense of accomplishment at using his skills as a lawyer to help someone find their true place in life.

"I want to give you a piece of my work as thanks." Kent ducked his head. "If you want one."

David said, "Show me what you've done."

They spent the next half hour looking at the sculptures Kent had finished. Some of them were already spoken for and others were slated for galleries. When David commented on the two he liked the best, Kent questioned him on why he liked them. Kent listened carefully; his whole self, engaged in the discussion.

"I've got an idea of your taste, so I'll make something specifically for you," Kent said.

David grinned at the younger man. "That would be awesome."

Kent asked, "How long are you going to be here?"

"Two weeks, two blessed weeks away from Seattle, my father, and my job."

Laughing, Kent said, "Well, I'll see if I can get it done in that time. If not, I can mail it to Seattle."

"That would be fine. Don't rush or ignore your other commitments on my account." David shook Kent's hand one more time and walked out into the bright sunshine. Everything looked a little more beautiful, with his satisfaction over Kent filling him.

CHAPTER FOUR

Lake Chelan

Jacqueline was thrilled to see Sandy manning the front desk when she arrived at the Anderson Bed and Breakfast. She'd pulled Betsy up in front of the lovely Victorian home, with flowers spilling everywhere and had felt the last tiny bit of tension ease away. She was going to have an amazing vacation; she could just feel it.

"Sandy, I didn't expect to see you here."

"I wanted to say hi when you arrived, so I told Mom I would be happy to take over the desk this afternoon. How was your drive? Did Betsy like it?"

Jacqueline giggled like a schoolgirl. Sandy looked up from the computer with a raised brow and Jacqueline blushed, she couldn't remember ever giggling as an adult. But she didn't care, she felt like giggling, or laughing out loud, or maybe even cheering. "Betsy loved it. It was a wonderful drive and the ride on the lake was so refreshing."

"It is. It's like everything negative slides right out of you as the ferry, or in your case the barge, travels up the lake."

"So, it isn't just me that feels like that?"

"Not at all. I think it's something magical. Tsilly doesn't allow negative emotions on his or her lake," Sandy said with a wink and a nod to the game she'd written, and they were still producing. The very game where the pornography had been hidden, to discredit the company.

"Well good for Tsilly, lake monsters need to keep control of their domain. We tourists need to chill, and what better place to do that than on Lake Chelan."

While Sandy got her all checked in, Jacqueline kept up a chatty conversation, telling Sandy about her tourist purchases in Chelan.

Sandy teased her about the baseball cap, saying only the tourists actually wore those. She'd been perfectly happy with that statement, because she was a tourist and didn't mind being an obvious one.

"And you're not going to believe it, but I bought two novels to read. Two!"

Sandy laughed. "That's awesome. If you need more, Mom keeps a bunch of books, in a kind of take one, leave one kind of arrangement. Most people don't want to carry back a book they've already read so a lot get left behind, which is why Mom started the idea."

"That makes sense, since a lot of people don't read as much at home, with work, family and home maintenance to keep up with. Why take them back to have them just collecting dust when someone else could enjoy them?"

Jacqueline let out a laugh. "But I cannot wait to settle in and read them. I plan to sleep late, read a lot, and take in some lake activities. I've been collecting those tourist brochures and will pour over them tonight, to see what I want to do in the two whole weeks I'm here."

She clapped her hands and spun around in a circle. When she was back facing Sandy, she knew her face was bright red. There was a man in the room behind her and he was quite attractive, from what she could tell by the glimpse she'd gotten, while spinning like a four-year-old. For Pete's sake, she'd been in town less than an hour and had already made a fool of herself. She wanted to hit her head on the desk or be swallowed up by a hole in the floor.

Sandy just grinned at her, then said, "David, come meet our newest resident."

The man came forward and winked at her, then stuck out his hand, "I'm David, nice to meet you. I heard you have big plans for our little town. Is that your amazing car out front?"

Jacqueline blessed him for changing the subject. He was even more gorgeous than she'd thought, but there was a kind light in his soulful brown eyes, that made him even more attractive. His almost black hair was mussed, and she wondered if that's what *lake hair* on a man would look like. He had a trimmed beard and a very kissable mouth. *Whoa, don't go there, sister, vacation, not moving here to be with the local boy.* "I'm Jacqueline and yes, that wonderful car is mine. Her name is Betsy."

~

David was absolutely fascinated by the beauty before him. When he'd walked in, she'd been leaning over the counter slightly, showing off her very fine ass in a pair of cropped jeans. She'd been going on and on about all her vacation plans and when she clapped her hands and spun around, he was lost. Her black hair had swirled around her and he'd caught a glimpse of a face worthy of a goddess. And it wasn't just her ass that was fine, her whole body was magnificent, worthy of her very own calendar. She was a pin-up girl in the flesh.

He'd gone stone still and couldn't think or move. By Sandy's expression and tone of voice, he'd realized the goddess had embarrassed the shit out of herself, and it was up to him to fix it. It had been him that she'd been embarrassed to find.

He'd noticed the classic car out front when he'd arrived, so he used that as a change of topic. Thank God it was hers. She grabbed the subject like a lifeline, the pink still high in her alabaster skin, which only made him want to... kiss her, throw her over his shoulder, ravish her... yep, any of those would do.

A smile tugged at the corners of her mouth, but her green eyes sparkled with delight. "Yes, that's Betsy. She's my pride and joy. My one true love."

One true love? Maybe he could change her mind on that. It would be magnificent to spend his vacation on that quest. "Well, Betsy is gorgeous. I assume you brought her on the barge and not the goat trail people keep saying is a road, down from the national forest."

"I did. I figured the drive from Seattle was enough for one day, so she took it easy on the barge. But she's a sturdy lady and would have made it down the goat trail if I'd asked her to."

Seattle, *hot damn*, maybe he could see this living, breathing Aphrodite after his vacation. "Most likely, they built them stronger, more reliable, back then. Can I help you carry in your luggage?"

She studied him in indecision for a moment and then said, "Well, thank you. That would be very nice."

The breath he was holding seeped out of him, that few more minutes with her seemed like a prize.

Sandy said, "David, can you show her where to park, too?"

He caught Sandy's eye and she winked at him. "Absolutely. It would be my pleasure." Turning back to Jacqueline he said, "Come right this way, lovely lady."

Jacqueline looked back at Sandy, who shrugged and said, "Vacation. Enjoy yourself."

Jacqueline's face turned beet red again, but she didn't argue. He had a feeling he'd just won some kind of prize. He sure as hell hoped it was more time with this gorgeous creature. With the way she was charging out of the house, he decided that his work was going to be cut out for him.

The woman was prickly, now that it was just the two of them. She started to unlock the trunk and when he laid a hand on her to stop, she about leaped out of her skin. He pretended like he didn't notice as her face flamed for the third time in as many minutes.

"It would be easier to drive around to the back and park, before unloading the luggage."

"Oh."

He gave her his best innocent smile. "That way I could ride in this magnificent car, even if it's only a few feet. If Betsy doesn't mind. I promise not to drool."

She relaxed, clearly the subject of her car was the way to, if not her heart, then at least her ease of interaction.

She gave him a half smile. "Betsy wouldn't mind, and I appreciate you not drooling."

That tiny, almost smile made him feel ten feet tall. His guess was she didn't used it often. He followed her to her door and held it open for her to get in and then hurried over to the passenger side.

"So, the driveway around to the back is behind Betsy, which means I could have a four-block ride in the lovely lady if you go around the block, rather than backing up."

Her almost smile was a little larger this time. "I can do that."

"I can hardly wait." David was not a huge car buff. To him, they were modes of transportation, but he could still recognize an amazing vehicle when he saw one. "What year is Betsy?"

She glanced to the side. "Not an enthusiast, then. Betsy is a 1956 Chevy Bel Air."

"Caught me, no I'm not an enthusiast, but I know beauty when I see it."

Jacqueline smoothed her hand over the steering wheel. "She is a beauty."

David agreed with the statement, but the woman behind the wheel far outshone the vintage car, at least in his opinion. She wasn't ready to hear that from him, but he planned to inch his way in, until she was.

"So, did you restore it, or did you buy it in this condition for a couple million dollars?"

She tensed, and he was afraid he'd stepped in the wrong direction, but then she pulled in a huge breath and let it out again. "My father and I restored it. It was a father-daughter project for many years and the best time I've had in my life."

She sighed again and said in a small voice, "He died before we finished it. Just literally days before the last part came in. We'd done everything else, but the rear-view mirror was cracked and we…"

Her voice trembled to a stop. David put a hand on her shoulder. "I'm so sorry. Sorry for your loss and sorry I asked."

"It's okay, the memories are all good ones, except for that one tiny bit. And it's been a year and a half now, so I need to get over it."

A tiny heart on the rear-view mirror sparkled and he envied her relationship with her father. "That's not a long time for grief with someone you loved so much. How long did it take to restore Betsy?"

She laughed but it still had a watery sound to it. "It took us eighteen years, three months and fourteen days."

David whistled. "Not a short-term project."

"Poor Betsy was a mess and we didn't have a lot of money to sink into her when I was young. Plus, we could only work on her on weekends most of the time. Some evenings if it was something small."

"Well, you and your dad did an excellent job."

"I almost sold her when Dad died. I was afraid I couldn't look at her again. But then the last part came in and I felt like my dad was there with me, wanting to see Betsy completed."

She glanced at him again as if deciding whether she wanted to continue. He held his breath hoping she would, praying she would.

"I got one of the detailing brushes and some red enamel and painted the tiny heart on the glass, then I went out and attached her to Betsy and I felt like I'd passed some kind of test. The love and the joy of the eighteen years plus filled me, and I knew I could never part with her."

He was so damn relieved to hear she'd worked through the sadness, and made, what to him, was the right choice. "I'm so glad you kept her. She's a very important part of your life. You must have started working on her when you were five."

Jacqueline chuckled. "Not quite but thank you for saying so. I was fifteen and starting to get interested in boys, so I think my father was being pro-active."

"Smart man." A quick calculation and he realized she was thirty-five to his thirty-one, he hoped she didn't have a thing against younger men.

CHAPTER FIVE

Lake Chelan

Jacqueline was completely mystified as to why she had told this complete stranger about her father dying, she had never talked about it with anyone. But not even five minutes with this man and she was pouring out her heart to him. That would never do. She didn't trust any man, every single one that she had ever counted on had left her, even her father had died.

She knew it was totally irrational to lump her father in with the worthless men she had dated, but she couldn't help herself. Even though he'd been gone a year and a half she still felt the sting of his passing. He'd abandoned her, plain and simple. The fact that he'd had heart issues and was on medication for it had shocked her to the core. Why hadn't he told her? Maybe then she would have been prepared for… no, she would never have been prepared. The simple fact was she needed him, and he was gone, all she had left was Betsy.

After he'd died, she'd realized that he'd been pushing to get Betsy done the last year. They'd spent longer hours in the garage, she'd not minded one bit, but she had noticed her father was very tired after each session, barely able to make it into the house. She'd scolded him and told him they needed to slow down. But then the next week he would seem fine and be raring to go again.

The doctor had finally told her, after his death, that his heart had been slowing down, giving out, and the only real cure would be a heart transplant, which he'd refused flat out, saying he was ready to go when God called him home. Well maybe he'd been ready, but Jacqueline certainly hadn't been. That was the whole reason she was still ticked off that he'd never told her and had just up and died on her.

She pulled into the parking area David directed her to and she knew when he leaped out of the car, he was planning to open her door for her, but instead of waiting and allowing him to be courteous she opened her own door and stood. She didn't want him treating her like that.

His good looks were already causing butterflies in her stomach. He was easily a foot taller than her five-foot, four-inch height. His linebacker shoulders and slim hips made her want to eat him up. The dark hair and earnest brown eyes made her feel giddy and turned her into a blabbermouth. But it was the beard outlining his very kissable lips that made her crazy. She wanted to grab him by his black hair and pull those lips down to hers and kiss him for a week or maybe two. Nope. She needed to nip this thing in the bud, she wasn't getting involved with a local boy. She wasn't getting involved with any man.

He gave her a sheepish look, when she stepped out of the car with an expression designed to fly the back-off flag right in his face. He didn't seem to notice and followed her to the rear of the car to carry in her suitcases. She wouldn't normally need help, but Sandy had said she would be on the second floor and Jacqueline was certain there was no elevator in the lovely Victorian home, so she would let Mister Linebacker help carry her rolling suitcase up the stairs. Then she would say goodbye and hope she didn't see him again during her two blissful weeks away from Seattle.

Even if Sandy's suggestion of having a vacation fling continued to echo in her mind, she was not going there.

∽

David was trying to figure out what made the lady tick. She'd told him all kinds of personal information and then had gotten quiet. Not quiet, silent, totally silent. When she was parked, he'd quickly hopped out of the car to open her door for her, but she beat him to it. She looked up at him with a suspicious glare, clearly trying to tell him to get lost.

He'd shrugged and tried to appear as innocent as he could. "Thanks for the ride in Betsy. Let's get your things in the house."

He followed her to the back of the car and nearly groaned as she bent over to unlock the trunk.

He was going to need a shower after helping the lady with her luggage, a cold one, a long cold shower to try to make him forget about the delectable woman he had followed up the stairs carrying fifty pounds of luggage.

Thank goodness he was in shape, due to volunteering with the paramedics in Seattle. He worked out nearly every night to keep fit and volunteered on the weekends. He didn't drive but he could help tote and carry, and he even had his EMT license, so he could assist on the calls.

When they reached her door, he was surprised and pleased to see she had the room across the hall from his own. She wouldn't be able to avoid him. He knew he should back off now, so he didn't look like some kind of stalker, so he set her bag on its wheels as she unlocked the door.

When her door was open, she turned back to him and he smiled. "Do you need any more help?"

"No, but thanks. You don't work here, do you? Like are you the bellhop?" she asked starting to open her purse.

He laughed and stayed her hand. "Nope, I don't work here. No tip needed. Having a ride in Betsy was reward in itself. See you around, pretty lady."

Then he turned and acted like he was going back down the stairs. He didn't want her to know he was across the hall until she was settled into the room. Then she would be less likely to ask Sandy for a different one. David didn't think there were any others open, but that was a chance he wasn't taking. When the door snicked shut and the lock turned, he quickly and quietly moved into his own.

He needed to plan how to engage the goddess across the hall. The touch of his hand on her soft skin had sent wild sparks through his entire body. Not once had a woman elicited those kinds of feelings, and he'd been out with plenty. She was either his perfect mate or they needed to engage in wild sex and get it out of their system. David had no idea which it was, but he was determined to find out.

CHAPTER SIX

Lake Chelan

Jacqueline was ecstatic to be starting her first full day of relaxing in Chedwick. She'd spent a pleasant afternoon getting settled in her room yesterday, looking through all her travel brochures and trying to decide what all she wanted to do. Then, Sandy's mom had suggested she get something to eat at Amber's café, so she'd done that. But the best part was she had read the first two chapters in her book.

This morning she slept late, well late for her, which was a decadent eight-thirty, then she padded down the hall to shower. There were four rooms on this floor that shared a bathroom, she didn't exactly know how to plan for that, so she carried all her bathroom items in the little travel bag and had grabbed some clothes. She'd seen towels last night on some shelves and a hamper to put the wet ones in.

She was almost to the door when it opened and none other than David walked out, freshly showered and wearing only jeans. Jacqueline stopped dead in her tracks, as she surveyed the hunky man standing in front of her. His chest and abs were beyond compare, and slightly damp, with a tiny amount of curly black hair running down his body, pointing to the promised land under his jeans, that were filled out in all the right places. His feet were bare and that was possibly the sexiest part of all.

Until she spied one water drop slowly making its way down his chest, she wanted to lick it off of him. Instead, she tore her eyes away from his chest and looked up into his laughing eyes. He bowed and waved his hand toward the door.

"It's all yours and I didn't even drain the hot water tank." Then he sauntered past her and walked down the hall while she stood there gaping at him. He turned and winked at her before going into the room directly across the hall from her own.

Jacqueline darted into the bathroom, her face flaming at her actions, and he, the rat, acknowledging them. Couldn't he have just ignored her stupefied behavior? No, he had to give her that wink to show her he'd noticed.

She set her toiletries and clothes down on the little table and looked in the mirror, what she saw in it made her want to scream. Her hair was in a lopsided ponytail, and there were makeup smudges under her eyes. She'd obviously not done a great job taking her makeup off last night. And the piece de resistance was her puffy face from sleeping so long. Lovely, just lovely, she'd always wanted to meet a sexy man in the hall looking like a clown or a ghoul, take your pick.

Sighing, she began her morning routine. Hey, wait a minute, what was David doing here at the B&B anyway? He said he'd grown up here, why was he in the hotel? She would have marched down the hall and asked him, except now her mouth was full of toothpaste and she was still looking like a ghoul.

Jacqueline was glad she hadn't followed her instinct to ask him, as she stepped under the hot water, it felt amazing and her thoughts cleared. There were a dozen possible reasons for him to be staying at the B&B, his house being worked on was the one that immediately popped into her mind, but she was sure there were others. Maybe he was buying a new place and hadn't quite got the dates lined up, or there was a delay. It was possible his wife had kicked him out and that's why he was being all flirty with her. Although she didn't think Sandy would have gone along with that one. It really wasn't any of her business and she needed to keep her nosiness to herself. But she did still wonder.

She'd decided last night that the first thing she wanted to do was scope out the town, maybe wander through some of the shops. Definitely the art museum slash craft store, and the costume slash wedding dress store next to it looked interesting. She had to wonder if all the shops in town doubled up on their purpose.

Jacqueline would love to go take a look at Sandy's brother's wood-working place. When Sandy lived in Seattle, they had all been jealous of the blanket chest that her brother had made, she'd love to see what else he did. So, her first day was firmly set on perusing the offerings in the town and maybe going to the lake to put her feet in the water, she'd seen a little park not far from the ferry landing that looked perfect.

She was giddy at the thought of having a leisurely day wandering the shops and town. She dressed in some shorts and a tank top because the weather indicated it was going to be hot today, much warmer than yesterday. The eastern part of Washington was nothing like the Seattle area, it was much more dry and hot, although in the winter it could also be dumped on by three or more feet of snow.

Living here would not be to her liking, she enjoyed the more temperate weather of Seattle and didn't really mind the gray and rainy days. That said, she was still going to enjoy the heck out of the sunshine, while she had the chance.

David grinned and mentally patted himself on the back for perfectly timing his shower. He'd thought he'd heard Jacqueline moving around in her room, so he'd hustled down the hall for a quick shower, hoping she would arrive for hers as he came out. He'd waited, listening for her door to shut, he'd noticed the day before that it had a small squeak to it, so he'd paused to hear that squeak, counted to three, and opened the door. Gratification filled him as she ogled his body, score one for some lust.

He'd decided last night that baby steps were going to be necessary, to ease himself into her plans. He wanted to take her out on the lake, maybe do some water skiing. Or up into the mountains by one of the rivers for a picnic. Chris had some nice rides at the *Tsilly Amusement Park* that they could get cozy on, and he assumed she would want to make at least one stop there, to see how Chris had implemented the different parts of the *Adventures with Tsilly* game that her company produced.

Sandy had given him lots of information when he'd quizzed her about how they knew each other, and he was thrilled to hear Jacqueline was Sandy's boss, and single. Sandy had even given him some hints about what her boss liked to do, saying she thought Jacqueline worked too hard and needed some fun in her life. David had been only too happy to volunteer for that position.

Today he was going to lay low and just casually bump into her here and there. Use that small-town card as much as he could. The main thing he worried about is if she'd signed up for something organized and would spend the whole day out of reach. He had no idea how to ask her about it either.

First things first, and that was breakfast. He waited until he heard her door open and shut twice, and figured she was on her way to breakfast, so he casually walked out of his room and followed her into the hall, where it was his turn to stop dead in his tracks. She was wearing very short shorts and had on a miniscule tank top in turquoise that he was certain would match her car. Her feet were in the sexiest sandals on the planet and her hair was up in a flirty ponytail that swung back and forth as she walked down the hall. He was certain he would start drooling any minute.

Thank goodness she hadn't seen him standing there staring like an idiot. Right before she got to the stairs she turned and gave him a sassy wink. The minx, she'd known he was there the whole time, and had been enjoying herself at his expense.

He laughed; paybacks were a bitch. Then he lit out to follow her into the dining room, where a plethora of food was laid out. Sandy's mom, Carol, came in from the kitchen with a fresh container of scrambled eggs. He was quite happy to scoop some up.

Carol asked, "Is there anything I can get either of you?"

David laughed. "There's enough food here to feed half the town. How many guests haven't eaten yet?"

"The family of four who are here for the amusement park should be down any minute, and the couple that are scoping out the town as a wedding destination haven't come down, yet. It's hard to say when they will emerge, young love takes precedence, you know."

David grinned at Carol; she'd taken to her role as a B&B owner like a duck to water. He had to wonder if she missed the hustle and bustle of the mayor's office she'd held for years and years.

She turned to Jacqueline and asked, "What did you decide to do on your first full day in town?"

Jacqueline glanced at him, then said, "I'm going to wander around town, peruse the shops, and see if Terry will let me come by his place and see what he's working on."

Carol grinned. "I can arrange that."

David frowned inwardly. Did she have something going on with Sandy's brother? Terry was a great guy, but he didn't see the two of them as being very compatible. Terry was, for lack of a better phrase, the class clown. Jacqueline seemed too reserved for someone like Terry.

The woman in question nearly grinned in pleasure and David felt red hot jealousy shoot through him, he didn't want her anywhere near Terry Anderson.

She said, "Thanks so much, Carol. I've always been envious of Sandy's furniture and I would love to have some of my own."

David relaxed. Furniture, his goddess wanted furniture. Terry did make excellent wood pieces. His place wasn't easy to find, maybe he could volunteer to show her the way.

Carol finished texting and said, "He'd be happy to show you around any time after four. You're lucky he's here this year, he's usually gone until mid-August making all his delivery runs, but they were all close to home this year, so he got back last week."

Jacqueline's eyes sparkled with excitement. "I can't wait. Where is his shop?"

David jumped at his chance, although he schooled his features and voice, to sound casual. "It's not very easy to find. I could take you out there about four if you want."

Carol frowned then nodded. "That actually would be a good idea. It is hard to find, the first time. David has been out to his place."

"Is it too rough for Betsy?" Jacqueline asked.

He said, "No, it's not rough at all, there are just a lot of twists and turns. Betsy would be fine, and I would love another ride in her."

"I think that's a good idea, we wouldn't want you getting lost." Carol put her phone back in her pocket and then cocked her head. "I think I hear the family coming. I'm going to refresh the juice; the kids love it."

David said, "Mind if I join you while we eat, then we can make plans to meet up and our breakfast won't get any colder?"

"By all means."

CHAPTER SEVEN

Jacqueline wasn't at all certain she wanted David's help to find Terry's shop, but she didn't want to get lost on some maze of roads either. So, she supposed he was the lesser of two evils, and she wasn't going to pass up seeing what Terry had on hand. Since he'd only been back a week, it might not be much, but maybe he had some things under construction.

She knew he took orders and made custom furniture, so seeing a catalogue of his work might be good as well. He had a very tiny web page, with only a few items on it. Even that was relatively new. She'd worked with Sandy for thirteen years, and only in the last five or six had their town gotten on board with web pages. How they had survived, at all, before that, was a mystery in her mind.

When they'd almost folded as a town six years ago, they'd finally realized they needed to do something. Sandy had told her about all the different things they'd done to save the town, and of course, since a lot of it was based on making the town a tourist destination, with the theme of the *Adventures with Tsilly* game, she'd known all about that end of things. So,

Chris had started the Tsilly Amusement Park, based off the *Adventures with Tsilly* game, that was then and still was now, quite popular.

Then they had opened the art gallery and a world renown glass artist had given them some of her work. She'd also heard some web designer had moved to town and he'd at least managed to drag most of the town's business owners into the twenty-first century and gotten them on the web. Finally, Carol and some of the other people had turned the town into a destination wedding place.

That's when Carol had retired from being mayor and had opened her B&B, and now the town was booming. The local economy had shot up and more people had moved in, to help staff the new businesses. Jacqueline was excited to see those new businesses, and she would take the help of David to find Terry's shop.

The man sitting next to her was definitely enjoying his breakfast, at least he wasn't one of those men that was uncomfortable with silence. He also wasn't the quiet brooding type and could hold his end of the conversation, as she'd found out yesterday. She was still feeling a little odd about blabbing her life story out to the complete stranger.

Jacqueline paused in her eating, and said, "So you heard I'm going to run around town and do some window shopping, and who knows, I might even buy something. A memento from my vacation maybe. So, if we could meet somewhere about three thirty, would that leave us enough time to get to Terry's by four?"

David grinned at her. "That would be perfect, and I don't think Terry is going to be watching the minute hand to make sure you're exactly on time, he's a pretty laid-back guy."

"All right, how about we meet at that little park I saw near the landing? I also want to maybe put my feet in the lake for a minute or two and I thought that looked like a good spot.

Although it might be filled with people; that Tsilly climbing structure has got to draw kids."

"It does, but I'll find you, it's a great spot for putting your feet in the water, there are some other locations around that are better for getting further into the water or even swimming. I could show you either on a map or in person."

Jacqueline wondered why he was being so helpful and also why he was available. "Don't you need to work?"

"Nope, I'm on vacation. I'll pop into a few places here and there, but my days are mostly free. I'm thinking about maybe getting in one of the excursions on the lake, a buddy of mine owns the boat, and there is everything from just cruising the lake to waterskiing available."

"Oh, that sounds like fun. I've water skied a time or two in Seattle, but just cruising the lake would be fun, too."

"I'd be honored to take you along when I go, if you want, or I can give you my friends info. He calls his company *Water Play with Tsilly*."

"Oh, I have a brochure on that. I was planning to find out more about it and book some time."

"Come with me then, I can get you a discount." He waggled his eyebrows. "I know the captain."

She smiled at his silliness and tried to decide if she really wanted to go with him. Jacqueline supposed it might be more fun with a local, and also going with someone she kind of knew. Wanting to think it over, she said, "I'll give it some thought."

"You do that. So, what other brochures did you pick up that you're contemplating?"

She reached into the front pocket of her purse and plopped a handful of them on the table.

His eyebrows rose. "Well you might need a little longer than a week to do all that."

"I'm going to be here two weeks. Two glorious weeks."

David nearly groaned at the excitement shining out of her eyes as she enthused over her two-week vacation. He had known she was off that long from overhearing her talking to Sandy, but he didn't want her to know how long he been standing there, like a statue, staring at her.

He picked up her brochures and started making two piles. "This is a must do. This is a meh, if you have time. Lady of the Lake is great, it basically picks you up where ever you are, and takes you all the way to the top of the lake, to the even smaller town than this one, named Stehekin, where you can take a bus ride around to see the sights. A lot of people start in Chelan and see the whole lake."

His goddess nodded. "But since we're already half the way up, then we can see the other half?"

"Exactly. This parasailing is better than that one. Safer, cleaner, and newer equipment, plus it's a little cheaper." He laid the amusement park brochure in the must-see pile. "I assume you plan to spend at least one day checking out the new rides. Two would give you more time to enjoy everything. Chris did a fantastic job in designing it and since you're familiar with the game it will be fun."

"How did you know I was familiar with the game." She had tensed up with that statement.

Shit, she didn't know he'd quizzed Sandy. Dumbass, he needed to keep his trap shut, although, if she knew it might be easier. "Oh, Sandy mentioned you were her boss." He turned his attention back to her brochures and sorted the rest of them. From the corner of his eye he saw she relaxed a tiny bit at a time—as he did that—while keeping up a running commentary on why he was sorting them as he did.

When he laid down the last one. He tapped the must-see pile. "Must see and do." Then tapped the other pile. "Meh."

She gathered up the two piles, pulled two rubber bands out of her purse, snapped them around the two groups, then put them back in her bag. He wondered why she had rubber bands in her purse. They weren't the kind used in hair, just plain old rubber bands. Women and their purses were one of the great mysteries in life.

He decided he'd pushed his luck far enough this morning and figured he better back off. His breakfast was mostly eaten so he pushed his chair back. "Gotta run. See you at three thirty at the park. Have fun shopping."

She looked a little startled at his abrupt departure, but he also caught a bit of relief in her eyes. Yep he'd nearly overstayed his welcome. He hoped after they went to Terry's, he could convince her to have dinner with him, so he didn't want to put her on the defensive now.

CHAPTER EIGHT

Lake Chelan

Jacqueline breathed a sigh of relief, when the little-too-helpful man walked out the front door. She couldn't quite tell if he really was just being friendly, like she'd heard people from small towns were, or if he had some kind of agenda.

Most men in her acquaintance had an agenda, so she knew she was leery of David. She didn't want to be rude, but she didn't need some man hovering around her for the next two weeks either. She wanted to do things on *her* timetable.

She was kind of glad he had sorted her brochures into the two piles, though. There were so many of them, every time she'd tried to decide what she really wanted to do, she got frustrated, and shoved them into a pile somewhere. She'd stuck them in her purse, to look at, while she was at the park with her feet in the water. Now she had a much smaller pile to go through and an idea of how long each one would take, several of them were all day excursions, so some planning would be in order.

Before stepping one toe out of the building, however, she needed to apply a second coat of her mega sunscreen. The first coat had had enough time to absorb, so it was time for the second. Jacqueline liked her skin, but in the summer, it was hard, she was either uber white or bright red, there was no such thing as a tan for her. She supposed she had her father to blame for that, bloodlines could be a bitch.

When she'd slathered herself with a second coat of sunscreen, she put it in her purse for later, waved goodbye to Sandy's mom, and went out to take Betsy on a cruise of the town. It wasn't a far walk to anything, but she would need Betsy if she bought something, and then later to go out to Terry's. But the primary reason was her skin, the less sun the better, especially the first few days. No merry jaunts for her. Even the walk from the car to the door of the shops would give her more sun than her skin was used to, primarily from working in an office building ten to twelve hours a day, but also from living in Seattle, where the skies were gray a lot more often than they were blue.

She took out her tourist map and aimed Betsy for the art museum and the costume shop next door. Pulling up in front of the art museum she rubbed her hands together in excitement, she could hardly wait to wander through the old Victorian house, to see what they might have.

A perky young woman met her before she managed ten steps past the door.

"Hi, I'm Mary Ann, welcome to Treasures, can I direct you to anything specific or do you want to wander?"

"Hello, Mary Ann, I want to wander, Sandy has told me all about some of the treasures to be found here."

"Oh, you know Sandy, how fun. Well feel free to wander and if you have any questions just holler. I'll be right over there in that little room working on charms and watching the munchkin."

Jacqueline looked in the direction she was pointing and saw a child that looked to be about a year old in a playpen.

The little girl was playing with two blocks, clacking them together and then putting them in her mouth.

"She's teething, so horribly drooly, right now. Why she likes the blocks I don't know, but Terry and Greg made them specifically for her." Mary Ann shook her head. "After they investigated for nearly a year trying to find the best possible wood, finish, style, and everything, for a baby to play with. Knowing they would go in her mouth. So, I am confident they are safe for her to drool on."

"Greg is Sandy's husband, correct?" She had no idea Sandy's husband had any woodworking skills, so she wondered if there was more than one Greg in town.

"Yes, and Terry is her brother. They are BFF's. All right, you didn't come in here to talk to me, so I will stop chattering your ear off and let you browse. Have fun!"

Jacqueline smiled at the cheerful young woman and took one more glance at the baby, she was a very pretty baby and Jacqueline felt a tiny bit of yearning for a child of her own. But she worked long hours, so a baby wasn't practical. She had a friend who was a single mom, deliberately, she'd not wanted to deal with a husband, so she'd had artificial insemination to get pregnant. Jacqueline didn't think she would want to do that, but her friend was perfectly happy and actually talking about doing it again to give her child a sibling.

It took her over an hour to see everything, going from table to table and room to room looking at so many fun things. She'd managed to keep her purchases under control, with only buying some soap and lotion made from the plants from this area, a gorgeous landscape that was a picture of the lake from a higher advantage point, and a pair of earrings.

Jacqueline went over to the cash register and laid everything on the counter along with her credit card. Mary Ann was immediately behind it with her baby on her hip. Up close the child was even more adorable. She held out her chubby arms to Jacqueline. She wasn't sure if she should take the child, so she hesitated.

Mary Ann laughed. "You don't have to hold drooly face. She's never met a stranger. I guess she gets that from me."

"I would enjoy holding her, if it's okay with you."

"Fine by me. I've learned to do almost everything one-handed, but it's easier and faster with two." Then she handed her baby over the counter.

Jacqueline took the child and gathered her in close, she didn't much care if the baby got her wet. She had that adorable child smell that went straight to Jacqueline's heart. She swallowed and asked, "What's her name?"

"Nicole Scottie, after the two people that helped me have her, right here in the gallery. She was an impatient little thing and the doctor, and her father, just barely got here in time. Nicole had been in town about twenty-four hours before she came in to look around and ended up being the one to sound the alarm."

Mary Ann chuckled and continued the tale. "I told her not to call the fire department, so she called pastor Scott, about the only other person she knew in town. Fortunately, he's one of the volunteer firefighters and has EMT training, so he could have delivered her if he'd had to. I made him look to see if she was crowning, because I felt the urge to push. She was, so we couldn't go anywhere. The doctor and my husband finally made it here, which got Scott and Nicole off the hook. But I still named her after them, because they helped me through the really scary part."

Jacqueline snuggled the baby close, she seemed to like the color of her tank top. She was pulling at the fabric wanting to put it in her mouth. Fortunately, it wasn't a very stretchy material, but baby Nicole had a death grip on it.

Jacqueline swiped the card, and Mary Ann wrapped up the purchases, as she continued the story. "After the trauma and everyone knew both me and the baby were fine, the firefighters thought it was hysterical, Scott being the notorious baby deliverer, so they made a giant cradle and put it on the lawn of the church. Nicole was living in the rectory next to the church at the time. Scott and Nicole are married now and will be needing a cradle of their own in about six months, not one that size, however."

"Well that's a relief, I don't think Nicole would relish having a baby that size." Jacqueline shook her head and reluctantly tried to hand the sweet child back across the counter. It took both of them to get her little fingers to unclench from Jacqueline's shirt.

"No, that would not be fun. It was like eight feet high. Ouch."

Jacqueline groaned at the thought. "I might be back I've got my eye on a couple of other things, but this is my first day in town for a two week stay, so I have to pace myself. If I bought everything that caught my eye it would be a year's salary."

"Oh, I so totally hear you on that. So many pretty things. I about went broke when we first opened."

Jacqueline looked back into the room. "Yeah, I need to make my escape before I give in."

"Awesome. Hope to see you again. Whether you buy anything or not."

"Oh, I will definitely buy something. I want one of the quilts, the problem is I love two of them, so I have to decide."

"Or you could have one for before the new year and one for after. Trade off every other year or every six months. Heck you could sleep with the air conditioner on all the time."

"You are so bad."

"I am, I really am." Mary Ann waved her away. "Go, flee, before you get trapped in my evil web."

Jacqueline laughed and made her escape. Mary Ann was a hoot and baby Nicole was adorable. She wondered if turquoise would be her favorite color when she grew up.

~

David was growing impatient, he'd looked at his watch every five fricken minutes for the last hour, and it was still forty-five minutes before he was supposed to meet Jacqueline at the park. He needed something to occupy his time, but he couldn't think of one single thing, he'd already done everything he could think of earlier in the day.

His first stop had been to talk to Fred about his boat excursions. A popular one was fishing, but Jacqueline didn't strike him as the fishing type, so they talked about some of the other ones he offered.

The sunset cruise was his favorite, David would like to take her out on it. Fred would pilot them over to the other side of the lake, so when the sun set it would reflect on the water. Often people brought a bottle of wine and a blanket to snuggle into when the temps dropped, and the breeze blew across the water. He didn't think she was ready for that yet, but maybe in a few days.

Fred also offered daytime fun, water skiing, and parasailing were two of the favorites. Plus, just tooling around on the lake. David was prepared for a discussion with Jacqueline of when and where they might indulge.

After his chat with Fred, he'd stopped by to see his mom and had stayed for lunch. He'd tried to talk her into going out with him, but she'd said it was silly to pay for a sandwich, when she could make one at home. The woman loved to fuss, so he let her.

But now he'd been waiting for what seemed like hours to go to the park and meet up with Jacqueline. He didn't want to go too early and disturb her time communing with the lake, but he couldn't think of anything to keep him occupied. He'd not been worried about filling the time on his vacation before he'd met the woman, so why now?

He'd planned to do some fishing, and some reading, and connecting with friends. He'd wanted to talk to Greg and Kent, but he'd already done that. He'd been busy that first day in town. David supposed that would end up being a good thing, if he could get Jacqueline to join him on excursions. That he didn't have anything on his plate he needed to get done, he hoped would work in his favor. But right now, he wished he had something to do that would fill the... thirty-eight minutes, before he could go to the park.

Inspiration struck and he charged off down the street. The lady would have been spending all day shopping and she might be thirsty. He went into the tourist trap that pretended to be a store and found an overpriced Styrofoam cooler. He grabbed a couple of water bottles out of the fridge along with a couple of other drinks, he had no idea what she might like, so he picked a couple of popular ones and then decided maybe he should get one or two diet drinks. Most of the women he knew drank diet all the time. He took that all up to the counter and paid for a bag of ice that would fill the cooler three times, especially after filling it with drinks.

After paying, he went outside. He put all the drinks in the cooler and covered them with as much ice as it would hold, and then looked around for something to do with the rest of the ice. Leaving it on the ground didn't seem right, nor did putting it in the trash can.

Finally, he saw a family dragging toward the store, they had a cooler on wheels, and he thought maybe they would like his ice. He walked over and smiled at the man. "I just bought this bag of ice, but my cooler is too tiny to hold it all. Would you folks like the rest?"

The man frowned at him. "We don't know you."

"I grew up here. The guy behind the counter can vouch for me."

"If you live here then why are you buying a cooler and ice?"

"I don't live here anymore. I live in Seattle, but my mom lives here so I came to visit. I'm meeting a friend in a few minutes, who's been shopping all day and I thought she might be thirsty."

The wife nodded. "That's really sweet of you and probably accurate. Take the ice, Jim. Then we won't have to buy a bag and throw half of it away."

Jim sighed. "Fine, we'll be happy to use it."

The wife smiled back at David. "Good luck with your friend."

David handed the ice to the man and lifted his own cooler. "Thanks. Have a nice day, folks."

How that woman knew he needed luck, David had no idea, did he look like he was worried? Or insecure? He didn't think so, but women picked up on things most men didn't. So, he would take her good wishes. Finally, his watch showed it was late enough to start walking toward their meeting location, if he walked slowly. Very slowly.

David did his best to slow down his steps, but when he wasn't consciously thinking about them, he would speed up. Finally, he just gave up and decided he would offer the drinks as a reason to be there early.

He got to the park and spotted her immediately, like she was a magnet and his eyes were iron filings. Jacqueline was sitting in the shade of a tree, her shoes next to her, like she'd had her bare feet in the water. She looked so pretty, almost picture perfect, and if he'd been certain she wouldn't catch him at it, he would have snapped a picture with his phone.

David was glad he hadn't surrendered to that urge,

because he'd only taken a few steps, before she turned her head and their eyes met and locked. He couldn't tell whether she was glad to see him or not, so he gathered an innocent air about himself and gave her his best smile.

"I stopped at the little store—which is really a tourist trap—and got some drinks. It's a warm day and I thought you might be thirsty. Shopping always makes me thirsty."

Jacqueline just looked at him for a moment and then her lips curved into what might be a slight smile. "I am a bit parched, thanks."

David breathed a silent sigh of relief; he'd passed this first test. "I've got water, some diet drinks and some fully loaded with sugar and caffeine drinks. Name your poison."

"Water would be perfect. Thank you."

He handed her a water and grabbed one for himself before sitting in the shade of the tree. "Did you enjoy your day?"

"Very much. The best was the art gallery, Mary Ann is a wild woman."

He grinned. "Oh yeah, she's a little firecracker for sure."

"She acted like we were besties from the moment I walked in the door. I even held her baby."

"Mary Ann has never met a stranger; her baby is a cutie." He'd seen pictures of baby Nicole. He wondered if he'd heard a little bit of yearning in Jacqueline's voice when she talked about the baby. He told himself that was a stupid idea, she was a career woman. An image of her holding a baby formed in his mind and it was a very intriguing image.

"However, I found it to be a very dangerous place."

Dangerous? The art gallery? "How so?"

"I could have spent a year's salary in there."

He barked out a laugh. "So dangerous to your wallet. Totally understandable. How much did it set you back today?"

She paused, and he realized it was a nosy question. "Sorry, I didn't mean to pry."

"No worries. I was trying to decide if I should tell you the amount for today or the amount it's going to cost in total. Because although I was circumspect in my purchases today, I will be going back and buying other things. I just bought these earrings and some lotion and soap."

"Pretty earrings and Iris's lotion and soap, I assume, she does make nice ones."

She sniffed her arm and he longed to sniff it too. "I loved the fragrance. Mary Ann told me a funny story about how she'd been going up to Stehekin to buy the soaps, that were being made right here in town, but no one knew. Oh, and I almost forgot, since I couldn't do anything with it right away, a very cool picture of Lake Chelan that's going in my house in Seattle."

"One of Rachel's?"

"Yes, it's amazing, it's at sunrise and the colors are wonderful."

He held his tongue since the only time the sunrise was vibrant is when there were fires in the area. Or at least that's what he'd witnessed.

"So, what else do you have your eye on?"

Her eyes sparkled and he almost didn't hear what she said next. "Well, there were two quilts I wanted, but I'm not going to buy both, even though Mary Ann suggested I should. She's good at her job."

David chuckled. "And so enthusiastic, you don't really notice."

Jacqueline pointed at him. "Exactly. Sneaky woman."

"Actually, she's not really, that's her true personality. You should have seen the way she drove before she had the baby. She probably could have papered her whole apartment with the speeding tickets she got."

"That really does not surprise me in the least. She seems to do everything full bore. No holding back."

"You probably wouldn't guess, but she's slowed down now, at least when the baby is in the car. She only gets about one or two tickets a week now instead of several every day."

Jacqueline laughed out loud, and the sound shot straight through him. She had an amazing laugh, deep and throaty, but he got the feeling she didn't use it very often. He vowed to try to make her laugh more often. Laughter was one of God's greatest gifts.

He looked at his phone. "Time to get a move on, lovely lady. We don't want Terry wandering off. He spends a lot of time in Greg's bar."

"Sandy's husband. I heard he has a law degree, I'm not a fan of lawyers, but it seems like kind of a waste."

Shit, what did she have against lawyers? "I think he uses that degree here and there, to help people out in town on a volunteer basis."

"Well that's noble, I suppose, rather than being a pushy jerk."

"Not all lawyers are pushy jerks."

A frown marred her forehead. "That's not been my experience so far, but I suppose only dealing with two it's not exactly a large sample."

"No, but it's hard to look past the two, especially if they were truly awful."

"They were, but I'm not letting them ruin my vacation by thinking about them. Let's go see some beautiful wood furniture instead."

Damn, he'd have to get to the bottom of this lawyer thing, but he could wait. "Since two quilts could not possibly cost an entire year's salary, you'll have to tell me what else you saw in the gallery."

CHAPTER NINE

Lake Chelan

Jacqueline regaled David with all the wonderful things she'd seen and wanted in the art gallery, as he directed her to Terry's shop. After about the fifth turn she was glad he'd come along, it really was kind of a maze of streets to get there. He was a good listener too and asked insightful questions. She normally didn't talk much about herself, but he had a way of drawing it out of her. Surprisingly enough, she realized she didn't mind.

"Turn left and then it's at the end of the road. You can't miss it now."

"Thanks. I'm glad you came along; I would have gotten lost. This is quite a warren of streets back here."

"It is. You couldn't get lost for days or anything, but it's not easy, that's for sure."

Jacqueline parked where David pointed and got out of the car. David had tried again to open her door, but she'd not waited, this wasn't a date. Maybe he was just being a small-town gentleman, but it still felt weird. She wasn't used to someone helping her out of her own car. She didn't mind in the least a man holding the door for her or helping her with her coat, but it was her car, so it felt odd to sit and wait for him to get to her side.

David pointed to a large barn-like structure where she could hear a saw running. She walked toward the door and didn't mind that David had put his hand at the small of her back. It seemed a little intimate, but she felt protected rather than controlled, so she didn't acknowledge it. It probably was also a part of his small-town upbringing.

He pulled the door open and ushered her into the building. The smell of wood and linseed oil assailed her senses. There was a faint smell of varnish and maybe paint thinner underlying it. There were stacks of lumber, Jacqueline was surprised to see they were stacked by kind. There were a half dozen or more projects in various stages of completion.

The walls were covered in drawings and plans, and one whole wall held a two-year calendar that spanned four full-sized white boards. The project plan was a heck of a lot more detailed than anything they had for their projects at the game company.

She didn't see a lot of windows, but it looked like mostly natural light, so she wondered where it was coming from, until she looked up, and found the whole ceiling was glass. She just stared at it in awe, until the whine of the saw ceased, and she looked across to see Sandy's brother pulling off his safety goggles.

He laid them down on the saw bench and grinned. Walking toward them he said, "You made it. David, thanks for bringing her out. I wasn't sure what Mom had planned for getting her here."

Terry held out a hand to David and then to Jacqueline. He shook David's and kissed hers. She rolled her eyes at his malarkey, she'd been told on many occasions, what a flirt Terry Anderson was.

Terry didn't seem to notice. "So, what exactly did you want to see?"

"Everything. What you've got going on, what you're starting. Pictures of previous projects. Anything you have for sale. And my little pseudo-engineer's heart wants to look at those plans on the white boards."

Terry laughed. "You sound just like my sister. I can have a room full of furniture and she's always drawn to the project plans. Well let's start there and get it out of the way so you will be able to actually look at the finished pieces."

"Excellent."

∼

David was largely ignored, as Terry flirted with Jacqueline. That kiss on the hand had infuriated him. He did not like it one little bit. Not. One. Little. Bit

Terry didn't seem to notice or care that David had gone rigid. Jacqueline hadn't been too impressed by the gesture, maybe Sandy had warned her about her brother's flirtiness. He followed the two around the shop for a while, then he found a chair to sit on.

He didn't really give a crap about the project planning, or want to look through the scrapbooks, or to have Terry gush on about something he was building and all the different nuances about it. To him it looked like a box—maybe a fancy box—but still a box. Terry called it a blanket chest and was describing in great detail all the wood he was using and how when he carved the design it would bring out the different colors of wood. Snore.

Terry was apparently a better salesman than Mary Ann, because when he was finally finished waxing on about the piece, Jacqueline pulled out her checkbook and wrote Terry a fat check. The man took the check from her hand and kissed it again. "Thank you for your patronage, pretty woman."

David clenched his fists and willed himself not to punch Terry in the nose. This time, however, he could see Jacqueline's face and all tension and anger fled, when he saw her roll her eyes at the flirt. Thank God she hadn't been pulled into the blond good looks of the man.

Terry didn't seem to mind in the least, he just grinned even bigger. David stood and went over to the two of them, pulled her hand out of Terry's grip and wiped off the place Terry had kissed.

Jacqueline laughed and said, "You snooze, you lose."

David had no intention of letting that gauntlet lie at his feet, so he pulled Jacqueline's hand up and kissed it in a slow sensual way.

When he was finished, Jacqueline looked awestruck, and she didn't roll her eyes at him.

Terry slapped him on the back in comradery. "Smooth. Let's go celebrate Jacquie writing me a fat check. I'll buy."

His goddess lifted one eyebrow. "Jacquie?"

Terry grinned. "Sorry, but Jacqueline is too big of a mouthful for this country boy. So, do you guys want to join me at Greg's for a brew and something deep fried? I imagine Sandy will be there, too."

David shook his head at Terry's malarkey and looked to Jacqueline to answer.

"I have heard a lot about the town's watering hole." She looked at David. "Shall we?"

The fact that she was asking him, thrilled him more than it should have. "Sure, why not."

"Awesome, give me two minutes to de-sawdust myself." He sniffed his underarm. "Make that ten."

Now David rolled his eyes. "We can meet you at Greg's."

"Okay." Terry turned off all the power and locked the

door. He glanced toward the parking lot. "Oh, my God. Is that a '56 Bel Air?"

Jacqueline nodded. "It is."

"Well, if I'd known you were driving that, I would have fought David harder." Terry walked like he was in a dream, staring at the woman's pride and joy. Damn, why did Terry have to be a car buff on top of a flirt, life just wasn't fair sometimes.

David followed the two of them again as they waxed on and on about the car. This was getting old, but he waited patiently, because he was the one getting in the car with the woman, not Terry.

CHAPTER TEN

Lake Chelan

Jacqueline, she just couldn't think of herself as Jacquie, had enjoyed her time at Terry's shop, and she was excited about her blanket chest. She'd wanted one forever, and her new quilt would be protected in the cedar-lined box. She was over Terry's malarkey, however, and she hoped Sandy would be at the bar to run interference.

It was one of the reasons she'd baited David, she kinda wanted to send a back-off signal to Terry, and she thought David would step up. She just hoped she hadn't gotten into something she didn't want, but she knew, in some ways, she did want to go that direction. She'd not been as attracted or as at ease like this with a man in, well, maybe forever, but certainly a long, long, time.

She'd thought about him all day, as she'd gone about enjoying the town, and when he'd shown up early to the park with a whole cooler of drinks, she'd been charmed. His interest in what she'd found shopping was so sweet, too. Most men didn't give a crap about a woman's interests, but he'd been a pleasant listener. Not just idly listening and letting her voice flow over him, but actually paying attention and asking her questions.

It had been a soothing balm, after dealing for so long with that stupid lawyer, that ignored everything she said and treated her like a moron, when she and Sandy were the experts.

Plus, David made her tingle. That kiss on the hand had sent fire licking along her veins and warmth pooling in her belly. She wondered what a kiss on her mouth would be like. She was seriously considering a vacation fling with the man, and she didn't even know his last name or what he did. Then she realized she really didn't care.

She only had two weeks in town, well twelve days now, so if she wanted to indulge, she would need to start. She knew she wanted more than one or two nights with him. Twelve days might be just about right to scratch this particular itch. Then she could go back to the city and leave the hot man behind.

She'd been following his directions and thinking. They pulled into the parking lot behind Greg's bar and this time she let him open her door for her. Things had changed between them and she was going to let them continue.

He took her hand and pulled her in close. "You let me open your door."

"I did."

"So…" He raised an eyebrow and looked at her mouth and then into her eyes.

"Yes, it means exactly what you think it means. I'm going to let you persuade me into your arms, and maybe even your bed."

"Wow. In that case can we go visit Terry again?"

Jacqueline laughed. "Kiss me, David, and then we'll go join your friends for a brew, and some really bad for us, food."

The man didn't have to be told twice, but he took his time. Lightly brushing his lips against hers, once, twice, three times. She raised up on her toes and pulled his head down for a firmer kiss. His lips met hers in a sweet, closed mouth kiss. She wanted more so she opened her lips, he took the hint, and his tongue swept inside to duel with hers.

He pulled her in closer, their bodies touched from chest to knees, and the heat ramped up. She wanted to drag him back into Betsy, she had a big backseat, it was filled with some of her shopping purchases, since the photograph was taking up most of the trunk. But surely, they could find a way.

Terry said, "Hey, none of that now, we're all going in for a brew."

They broke apart and both of them looked at Terry standing there grinning at them. She wanted to push him away, but decided they probably needed to slow things down a bit, she'd only known David about thirty hours and here she was plastered against him.

Apparently, David had come to the same conclusion because he moved back a little and said, "Fine, if you insist."

Jacqueline felt bereft of the warmth David's body had afforded her. She sighed as he pulled back further. Then he looked at her. "This isn't over."

She poked him in the chest, it was rock hard and nearly hurt her finger. "It better not be."

Terry slapped David on the back. "Come on you two, I've got a powerful thirst."

David frowned. "Yeah, me too and you just interrupted mine being quenched."

Terry laughed and grabbed her arm. "Come on, beautiful, before Mister Thirsty starts up again."

She let Terry pull her along, but she reached out and caught David's hand, and the three of them went into the bar where there was laughter and music, beer, and fried foods galore.

∽

David was slightly relieved that Terry had come upon them making out in the parking lot. He'd been about two seconds from tugging Jacqueline into the back seat of Betsy and then all bets would have been off. So, before they put on a show for nearly every resident in town, it was good Terry had put a stop to the craziness her lips had started on his. He was all on board for some naked fun, but back at the B&B was a whole lot better place than in the parking lot, of the only hot spot in town. It might be Sunday night, but that didn't stop many people from hanging out before work the next morning.

David was glad Jacqueline didn't just let Terry pull her into the bar, but had latched on to him to drag him along. If he didn't know Terry well, he might be tempted to punch him in the nose, but he did know him, so he just followed along.

He was doubly glad he'd worked things out with Greg, so he didn't feel unwelcome. Once they were inside, Terry made a beeline to where his sister was sitting.

Sandy looked at her brother who still had a hold on Jacqueline. "Is there a reason you're dragging my boss around, brother?"

Terry let go of Jacqueline and grinned at his sister. "Not dragging, escorting. I was escorting your boss."

Sandy raised an eyebrow. "Looked like man-handling to me."

Then she looked at Jacqueline. "Feel free to smack him."

"If I need to, I will. Thanks for giving me permission."

Finally, she looked past both of them and said, "Hi, David."

"Hi, Sandy."

"Looks like my boss was tugging you along, too."

He laughed and decided not to comment. He liked Jacqueline pulling him along in Terry's wake. When Jacqueline tried to pull her hand away, he squeezed her fingers to let her know he was happy to have her holding his hand. Then he released her and pulled a chair out for her to sit, then sat beside her.

Terry asked, "What does everyone want? It's crowded tonight, so I'll go get us drinks to start with. Sandy, we haven't eaten yet, so clue them in on what Greg has, we'll let Jessica take our orders for that. I want chicken fingers and fries if she gets here, before I get back."

When Terry had left with their drink orders, they chatted about the menu, basically anything and everything that could be deep fried. Obviously not somewhere a person wanted to eat often, but once in a while, it wouldn't kill him. Once they'd made their minds up, David sat back and enjoyed listening to the women discuss their day.

Jacqueline waxed on about both the art gallery and Terry's shop. She'd liked some of the other places as well and planned to get some of Samantha's fancy cookies to take back at the end of her vacation for the development team in Seattle. Samantha had cookies that went along with the game theme and Jacqueline was sure the devs would get a kick out of them.

Suddenly Sandy sat up straight and looked at Jacqueline. "Hey, can I ask you a huge favor? One of the cars for the Fourth of July parade isn't going to be able to participate. Would you mind driving Betsy with some local celebrities in the back seat?"

Jacqueline nodded. "I could do that, in fact, I brought one

of my favorite red, white and blue outfits in case there was a party or something. It's one I dress up in when I take Betsy to car shows, so it's kind of a vintage pin-up girl look."

David was all on board with seeing Jacqueline in a pin-up girl outfit. So much so he thought he might drool at the very idea. If he'd been a dog, his tail would have been wagging a mile a minute. Thank God he wasn't a dog, so he could at least pretend to be cool.

Jacqueline looked at him and asked, "You want to ride with me?"

"Hell, yes." Okay, cool he was not. Or smooth.

Jacqueline laughed and the sound skittered through him. That was twice he'd gotten her to laugh today, both times were an absolute gift. He loved the way that woman laughed and since she did it so rarely it was doubly powerful.

Terry arrived back at the table with brews for the men and a rum and coke for Jacqueline. Sandy was already nursing a glass of wine. "So, did Jessica come by yet? Did you order? I'm starving."

"Forget to eat lunch again, brother?"

"Yeah, was busy with a project." He looked around and waved at Jessica.

Jessica walked up to the table. "You already have drinks, so I take it you forgot to eat lunch again today, Terry."

"Yes. So, can we order? I'm starving."

Jessica put a bowl of peanuts and pretzels on the table and then took their orders, while Terry crammed his mouth full of the snacks.

"You need a keeper, Terry Anderson."

Terry swallowed and said, "You applying for the job, Jess?"

"Oh, hell no. Do I look stupid? No, I do not. I'll get your order in." Jessica turned and flounced off.

David wanted to howl in laughter, especially since he knew they'd gone out a time or two.

Sandy said, "Well, she has your number and it's been crossed out with black sharpie."

Terry laughed at himself along with the rest of them. "What can I say, I'm loveable, but not very dependable or self-sufficient. I can plan a build schedule like nobody else, and can accomplish it, but eating or remembering to pick up a date on time, or at all, not so much."

Jacqueline asked, "So did you remember we were coming to your shop today at four?"

"Yes, I did, just as soon as I saw you standing there."

David snorted and Jacqueline shook her head.

Terry just raised his hands and shoulders in a bemused shrug.

When their food came out there was an extra plate and David wondered if Terry had ordered two meals, but then Greg showed up with another round for everyone and a beer for himself. He kicked Terry's chair and said, "Scoot over."

"Fine, you big bully." Terry pulled his chair over closer to Jacqueline.

"My bar, my wife. I do what I like."

CHAPTER ELEVEN

Jacqueline thoroughly enjoyed the interaction at the table. She didn't have any siblings and had moved across the state, from her hometown, so she had friends but not lifelong ones, like these seemed to be.

She'd met Greg once or twice but seeing him in his home environment was a completely different experience. He'd always appeared to be rather quiet and withdrawn. He still wasn't exactly the life of the party, that was obviously Terry's job, but he was friendly and relaxed.

She sensed something between Greg and David, not adversarial, but not completely relaxed either. More like they were getting to know each other, which seemed strange to her.

When they had finished eating, and Greg was getting ready to go back behind the bar, a shrill tone sounded. The music was slapped off and everyone quieted, while a voice spoke over the crowd.

"Boating accident on the lake, multiple injuries, all medical personnel needed at the landing."

Greg looked around the table. "Terry, just your second

beer, right? David, you too? Can you give us a hand, your big city EMT training will come in handy?"

Both he and Terry nodded. David and Terry stood and moved quickly toward the parking lot.

Greg stood and spoke, "Anyone that's had less than two drinks and has EMT status, let's roll. The rest of you stay here and get sober, just in case, we'll have dispatch tone it out again if we need more hands."

When Greg and a few others had left the room, the music came back on and Jacqueline looked at Sandy for explanation. She'd never seen anything like that.

Sandy said, "We have a volunteer fire department, so if the guys are needed, the dispatcher sends that shrill tone and tells what is required. Greg is assistant fire chief, so the volunteers answer to him, he's extremely strict about drinking and answering calls. We've got one doctor and one nurse in town, so when there are multiple injuries like the dispatcher said, then the first responders do what they can. Most of them have EMT training. David has a bit more from working on an ambulance in Seattle, starting when he went to UDub, so his skill is valuable."

Jacqueline was surprised to hear that David had attended the University of Washington. It was a great school, but there were some good ones in Eastern Washington also.

Sandy interrupted her thoughts. "With the guys gone, do you want to hang around here, or do you want to come over to my house for a while and chat?"

Jacqueline wasn't much of a bar person, and with the men busy, she saw no reason to stay. "Let's go to your house."

"Great, I walked here, so do you want to drive Betsy over, then when you're ready to leave you'll have your car?"

She'd only had the one drink and a couple sips out of the second, so she wasn't worried about driving. "Sure, I could use some quiet. What about the bill?"

"Greg will take care of it."

Jacqueline wasn't quite sure what that meant, but Sandy wasn't concerned, so she decided she wasn't either.

~

David was exhausted. Those fools on the lake had really torn themselves up. He'd learned after he'd stabilized three of them and the doc had taken them away, that they'd been drinking and driving fast on the lake, in the dark. Apparently two boats had been racing and they'd plowed into a third, one that hadn't even been moving. It was a houseboat and the family on board had been playing a game below deck.

Fortunately, no one lost their lives, but there were some serious injuries. David had given the father of the family his card and had said he would be happy to represent him, pro-bono.

He was pissed off at those dumb asses, so if he couldn't calm down about the accident, and the family did request his services, he might have to pass it off to a coworker, but he knew just the one that would be perfect.

He, Terry, and Greg drove back to the bar, much, much later. They had blood on their clothes and a piss poor attitude. He hoped that Jacqueline was back to the B&B and in her bed. He was not in the mood for romance. His heart hurt from the pain that family was going to go through, because some damn assholes had been acting a fool.

When they saw Jacqueline's car was gone, Terry drove him to the B&B after dropping Greg at the bar to close up, or at least get his truck.

Terry said, "What a fucked-up way to end a fun night."

"Yeah, you got that right. Hope pastor Scott and his dad can give the family some peace and courage. They are gonna need it."

"That's an understatement, but if anyone can, they will find a way to get it done. I saw you give the dad your card. If they call you, roast those drunks."

David unclenched his jaw and fists. "It will be my pleasure. Assholes, what in the hell is wrong with people? Just decide to get drunk and cause a catastrophe for a completely innocent family."

"Yeah, I hear you, and their crappy actions ruined the night for the whole town, because we have to clean up their mess. Jerks."

David doubted he was going to be able to let this go quickly. A long, hot shower to wash the blood off might help him relax, but his mind was going to be seeing that hurt family for a long time. He sighed and said to Terry, "Thanks for the ride. Try to get some sleep."

Terry shook his head, probably thinking it would be a long night for him as well. "Yeah, you too."

David dragged inside, not physically tired, but emotionally, he was toast. It never got easier to see innocent people hurt by the actions of others. He went directly to his room to peel off the clothes with blood on them and stuffed them into a plastic bag he always carried when he traveled, then headed for the shower. He turned it on as hot as he could stand, hoping the hot water would wash away the sorrow, along with the blood and disinfectant.

He pulled on a pair of gym shorts and padded down the hall. Jacqueline stepped out of her room, she looked so gorgeous, but he didn't have the energy for her right now.

"I'm sorry I bailed on you."

She walked into his arms and gave him a hug, that started to thaw the knot of anger in his chest. "Don't be, other people needed you. I went with Sandy and we listened to the chatter on the radio. Sandy has the frequency the guys use to communicate unofficially. She said Greg sounded pissed."

"Yeah, it was awful."

"Want to come in just for a moment and tell me about it?"

He almost said no that he didn't want to talk about it, but he felt his head nodding. Jacqueline took his hand and pulled him into her room and guided him to one of the chairs that sat in front of a fireplace.

She poured him a shot of Jameson's. "Sandy sent this home with me; said you might need it."

"Sandy's a smart woman." He took the drink and gulped half of it down. The burn of the liquor continued the slow thaw. His mouth started talking, before he realized he did need to talk about it. "A couple of drunks decided to race their boats in the dark. Because they were drunk and looking at each other, rather than what was in front of them, they plowed into a houseboat that was anchored. The guy in the lead clipped the back of the boat sending it spinning into the other guy."

"Oh, no."

"That's not the worst of it. The family inside the houseboat was playing a board game, below deck. The only thing that saved them from drowning, is that a lake security officer saw the idiots racing and was coming from across the lake. Their quick thinking saved the family. All four had major injuries, as did some passengers on the two idiot's boats."

"Oh, my God."

"No lives were lost, but there were injuries that are going to change some futures, at least in the short term. The family taking the brunt, of course. Fuck. We did our best but, well it just sucks." David put his head in his hands, the futility of the whole situation was astounding. Two men showing off, dammit.

Jacqueline came over and sat on his lap, she put his arms around her and hers around him. She kissed his forehead.

And then soothed his frown with her fingertips. One hand kneading the tight muscles in his shoulders.

"You did all you could. It might not turn back time, but you being there saved lives. That family has a chance to heal and grow because you and the other guys stopped your own activities and went to their aid."

"I know, but—"

"No buts. You're not God, you can't change the actions of others. Even God doesn't stop people from making bad choices, short of lifting that houseboat out of the water and placing it in another location, the crash was inevitable. Those two caused much pain and suffering with their own stupid actions."

Jacqueline lifted his face up to hers and gave him a sweet kiss, which finally thawed the rest of the coldness in his chest. She was right, his job was to help where he could, that was all he could do.

He let her sooth him, the tension flowing out of his body with each gentle caress, until his muscles had all relaxed and he felt his mind letting go, too. He was nearly asleep, but knew he needed to go back to his own room for the night. "I should go. I, um, don't want our first night together to be less than perfect. If you're still interested in a night together."

"I am, but I agree, not tonight." She got off his lap and he felt the loss keenly.

He stood and pulled her into his arms. "Thanks, you helped. A lot. I'll see you in the morning. Maybe we can find something fun to do."

She smiled and raised up on her tip toes. "Maybe we can." Then she pulled his head down and gave him a gentle kiss.

The kiss filled his body with warmth, and he wished he had the fortitude to take it to the next level, but he didn't, so he hugged her tight. Then whispered, "Tomorrow."

CHAPTER TWELVE

Jacqueline hoped that she had helped David to let go of his anger and get some sleep last night. She was ready for the day and was looking forward to maybe spending it with David. She didn't know if he would have anything else he needed to do about the accident, and she kind of doubted he would be ready for a lake adventure.

Sandy had mentioned that there were a lot of great picnic spots near the two rivers. Jacqueline had seen in the tourist brochures that Amber made picnic baskets, that could be picked up and taken with them. Or there was also the amusement park. She did want to spend a day or two in there.

She had propped her door open a slight bit so she could see when David was up. He popped his head in the crack. "Are you waiting for me?"

"I was. Are you ready to face the day?"

"I am, and I smell something wonderful drifting up the stairs." He sniffed the air like a hound dog. "I'm starving, may I escort you to the dining hall, pretty lady?"

Jacqueline smiled at his foolishness, apparently, he'd set

the trauma of last night to the side and was attempting to be charming. She thought that was a good idea, not that he wouldn't revisit the frustration and anger he'd felt, but there really was nothing else he could do at the moment.

They walked down the stairs hand in hand and into the dining area, where Jacqueline had to admit there was something, besides the coffee, that smelled wonderful. A frittata maybe? She hadn't realized she was hungry, since she'd been trying to find an activity for them to do away from the lake.

They went through the buffet and filled their plates with an array of tempting food, and carried those, and mugs of coffee, to a table in the corner next to a window, with a pretty view of a small garden.

"So, I was looking through my tourist brochures and wondered if a picnic up on one of the rivers might be fun. Or there is always the amusement park."

David looked at her and smiled sadly. "Thanks, staying away from the lake for a day or two would be nice. It will take them some time to clean up the boat wreckage. Do you have a preference on which thing to do? I think Hank also will rent out a couple of horses for people that want to take a trail ride. He doesn't advertise it, because it's a working ranch and he doesn't want to turn it into a dude ranch, but word of mouth is powerful."

"Let's pass on the horses. I think a picnic and maybe a little hiking near the river sounds the best. I'm up for a leisurely day. I hope it doesn't sound presumptuous, but I called Amber's restaurant and ordered us a picnic basket. I figured we could use it, regardless of what we decided to do."

A slow smile slid across David's face. "Presume away, I am totally on board with whatever suits you."

"You don't need to go by the police department, or anything do you?"

A flicker of anger shot through his eyes, but it was gone

quickly, and he shook his head. "No, we gave our statements last night, and police chief, Nolan, said he would call if he had any questions."

"I didn't know which river or picnic spot was the best…"

~

David was thrilled that she'd started making plans to spend the day with him, before he'd had time to mention it. "I can help with that. Do you want to take Betsy to enjoy the outing?"

"I think Betsy would like that. Unless you wanted to drive."

David knew he was going to need to come clean soon, and explain to her that he didn't live in town, and he was a lawyer, and he'd flown in and didn't have a car with him, although he could borrow his mom's if he needed one. But he just wasn't ready to have to explain it all. Jacqueline seemed to like the idea of him being a local boy and having a vacation fling.

When she found out he wasn't local and in fact lived in the same town she did, but even more importantly, that he was a lawyer, she might not be so friendly. So, he was going to wait on that until he didn't have a choice.

"Nope, no need for me to drive, besides I like cruising around in Betsy. She sure gets some looks from people."

"She does, I'm looking forward to the parade."

He barked out a laugh. "Ha. I'm looking forward to the pinup girl costume."

She leaned in close. So, he leaned too. "I think you're going to love it."

The look in her eyes caused heat to rush through his body, and he realized he needed to find some condoms, quick, before they got too much further down the road that look was pointing to. He'd not had any idea he might need some while on vacation in his hometown. But apparently, he would, and soon.

He didn't want to be obvious about it however, so he was trying to think of a way to slip off for a minute, the tourist trap they called a store had plenty of them. And a blanket to take with them to sit or lay on would be handy too. He still had the little cooler to put some drinks in. Maybe he could use that as an excuse. The store wasn't far from Amber's so he could go there while she grabbed the picnic, although that wasn't very gentlemanly. What a conundrum.

They finished breakfast and grabbed some sweaters, because even though it was summer and hot out, one just never knew when a breeze or storm might slip over the mountain and catch people that were unprepared. David got some ice for his little cooler and they headed out, now that he knew what she liked to drink he could buy the right things.

Jacqueline pulled up in front of the restaurant, before she could get her car turned off her cell phone rang. She looked at it and groaned. "I have to answer this."

"I'm going into the store down there for drinks and then I'll get the food, you take your phone call and relax."

She nodded and answered her phone, while he hustled down the street to the store for supplies of several kinds. Jacqueline was still on the phone when he went into Ambers.

"Hi David, do you want a table?"

"No, I'm here to pick up the picnic Jacqueline Hurst ordered. She got a phone call just as we pulled up." He waved to the front where he could see just the front bumper of Betsy.

"Oh, that's her classic car, what a treat, it's mostly men that like the classics."

"Yep, her car, she and her father restored it. She says it was her dad's way to keep her mind off boys."

Amber grinned. "What a smart father. I'm going to mention that to Greg for when he has kids. Much better than him glaring and brooding. Jeremy will just write the boyfriends into a book and kill them off."

He chuckled. "Well since your first one is a male you've got time before you need to worry about boyfriends, plus an older brother can be a nice deterrent. Do Greg and Sandy have plans for that anytime soon?"

"Not that I've heard, but you just never know, now do you? Let me get the picnic."

While Amber hurried off to get their food, he again pictured a little baby in Jacqueline's arms, one with her porcelain skin and dark hair, he could almost picture himself right there looking on… and he was getting way ahead of himself.

But the picture of the three of them stayed fully embedded in his brain, and it even added a second older child, on his hip. For the first time ever, the idea of kids didn't scare the crap out of him, and he assumed part of that, was due to his therapist helping him to realize he wasn't his father, and didn't have the same personality or proclivities.

The other part of it was Jacqueline, she hardly even knew him, but had managed to soothe him last night, enough that he had slept well. He'd called the clinic first thing to find out about the family, and had been assured they had a restful night, and were on the mend with no foreseeable complications.

He put the food and his purchases in the back seat of Betsy and noticed Jacqueline had her head back against the headrest. He slid into the front seat and she just sat there rigid.

"I take it the phone call was not a happy one."

"Ha, way beyond not happy. That son of a bitch lawyer pulled some damn thing in court, where all they were going to do was sentence the jerk who tried to sabotage the game. It was a done deal, and now it might not be anymore. Why would he do something like that?"

Jacqueline turned toward him. "It was over. Months of dealing with the misogynistic jerk, why did we get a lawyer like that? I ask you, why? He's supposed to be working for us. But no, Sandy and I aren't intelligent enough to listen to. It's only the men in the company that know anything. Well, she and I were in the trenches, not the upper level muckity-mucks, who finally took the jerk out to play golf, and then he at least did his job. Until today. Why did he deliberately go in and delay the sentencing? Is he getting a kick back from the other company? Or is he just trying to eke out more time, so we have to pay him more? I just don't get it, maybe it's my feeble little female brain, but it seems fucked up to me."

David didn't know what to say, this was sounding a whole lot like a case he knew his father was working on, and the lawyer in question was sounding a whole lot like his father. No wonder she hated lawyers.

She sighed. "Sorry, I know you can't do anything about it, and I don't expect you to. I just had to vent."

He wasn't completely convinced he couldn't do anything, but now was not the time to discuss that. He needed a chat with dear old dad first. "So, do you have to go back to Seattle?"

"No. I refused. They can wait two weeks until I get back. I am not derailing my vacation because of some know-it-all jerk. But the Monday after I get back, is a completely different story. A three P.M. meeting is planned. Dammit. I couldn't have one day back before the drama?"

He took her hand and unclenched the fist, finger by finger, then he raised her palm to his lips and kissed it. He scooted closer, *gotta love the bench seats from back in the day*, and took the other hand, repeating the process.

"Let's go sit by a stream and relax. I'll give you the shoulder massage this time. And we can both put all our worries and concerns on the back burner. They won't go away, but they don't have to ruin our picnic either. Plus, I was thinking of an out-of-the-way location where the cell coverage can be spotty, so we'll have an excuse not to answer our phones."

Jacqueline nodded and reached forward to start her car, her hands were shaking a bit, but he didn't think that would keep her from driving safely. "Sounds perfect."

She followed his directions and they arrived at the little nook he'd picked. There didn't seem to be anyone around. It was not easy to find for the tourists, and the locals were mostly all at work, so he didn't expect anyone to intrude on the idyllic location.

CHAPTER THIRTEEN

Lake Chelan

Jacqueline parked Betsy where David had told her to and followed him down a short path to a small clearing next to the stream. There was plenty of shade for her uber white skin. David carried a lot more than she'd been expecting him to. He'd put the drinks in his little cooler and had a blanket and the picnic. She carried their sweaters and the tiny backpack she'd brought with keys, sunscreen, sunglasses, and a foldable sun hat. It also held one of the novels she'd bought, and her phone.

David set down the food and started to lay the blanket down in the sunshine.

"David, can you put at least part of the blanket in the shade? My skin doesn't tolerate sun very well."

"Of course, it never even occurred to me, so that's why you were under the tree at the park." He quickly moved to the shade and laid out the blanket.

"Yes, I can only be in the sun for a few minutes, so after I splashed in the water for a little bit, I had to get out of the sun. My uber white skin can be a pain. Even in the shade, I'll have to put on some of my heavy-duty sunscreen every couple of hours. I already applied it back at the B&B."

"Well for what it's worth I think your skin is amazing and I will be more than happy to help you reapply the sunscreen." He waggled his eyebrows at her.

She giggled at him. She couldn't remember the last time she'd giggled. Jacqueline Hurst did not giggle, but she just had. Oh no wait, she'd giggled just two days ago, who was this giggler?

He grinned at her like she'd handed him a million dollars. "Now that's a sound I would like to hear more often."

She rolled her eyes at him but wondered if he did have the power to bring out a more playful Jacqueline. One that might giggle and let a man call her Jacquie. She'd not felt playful in… well no less than a year and a half, maybe longer.

Before she sat on the blanket, she walked over to the stream, which up close, was a lot bigger than it had looked from the path. They'd gone up in elevation so she thought it might turn into a full river down lower on the mountain.

David arrived by her side. "You could put your feet in the water, but it will be cold. It's still snowmelt this time of year. By next month it will be warmer."

She bent down and touched the water. "You're right, it is cold. I think I'll pass on putting my feet in. Even the lake was cool."

"Yeah, it's deep, so it doesn't heat up a lot. If we go out for some water sports it might be wise to use wetsuits. Especially with your skin, it will keep the cold *and* the sun off."

"The stream is really pretty, though." She pulled out her phone and took a couple of pictures. "Hey, my service is strong up here. You said it would be spotty."

His expression was pure devilment. "I lied, but you can tell everyone in Seattle that it was spotty, they won't know the difference."

Jacqueline laughed and shook her finger at him. "That's just wrong, but I love it."

He took hold of her finger and kissed the tip. "Voicemail is a wonderful invention."

That tiny touch of his lips on her finger sent sparks through her body. She ignored them, as best she could. "True, and if it annoys the boss, then so be it. I'm on vacation."

David pointed at her. "Hey, I thought you were the boss."

"I am, but there's always another one higher up."

"Isn't that the truth." He shook his head sadly. "But we're both on vacation, which means for another twelve days we have no boss."

"Yay!" Jacqueline plopped down on the blanket and pulled off her shoes. She rolled her sweater around her tiny backpack and made it into a pillow and laid back onto it.

"I'm just going to lay here and look at the trees and the blue sky peeking between the branches, and listen to the water splashing down the hillside, and forget all about any cranky people. And you need to do the same, forget about drunk and irresponsible idiots. We'll just put the world on hold for a few hours."

~

David decided that her suggestion sounded like heaven on earth, and he was more than happy to comply. He couldn't fix a damn thing right now, so he sat down beside her, took off his shoes, bunched his sweater into a wad, and laid down beside her.

She took his hand and he was happy to let her hold it for as long as she wanted to. Peace filled him and he sighed, he heard her sigh at the same time. It was pleasant up here, with her by his side. In fact, it was nearly magical.

They laid there, side by side, chatting about inconsequential things. TV shows they liked, movies, and their taste in books. She liked thrillers and historical romance, and he liked horror and mysteries.

They were both only children, so they talked about that for a while, and both of them thought it was a lonely way to grow up. They didn't stay too long on that subject, because there was an air of intimacy surrounding it, that he didn't think they were ready for.

Their food tastes aligned better than their entertainment preferences. They both liked to cook some of the time, but also liked to go out. He told her about his specialty dishes, and she did the same. Both of them expressed they would like to sample the other's signature meal.

Once they had hashed out all their food proclivities, they decided that all that talking had made them hungry, so they pulled out their picnic lunch. Amber did a great job on a portable meal, and he'd felt it had been a very reasonable price for all the food they got.

As they ate, he told her all he'd found out about the boat trips Fred offered. They decided on a couple of them and also talked about visiting the amusement park. They didn't plan every minute for the rest of their vacation, but they put a nice chunk into it. The July 4th celebration and parade would be one whole day, with fireworks over the lake at night.

"So, we're going to live in each other's pocket for the next twelve days." She smiled a shy smile. "Are you certain you want to do that?"

"I honestly think I could live in your pocket for a whole lot longer than that."

"Maybe, but let's not push our luck. One day at a time is good."

He moved a little closer and drew her into a warm kiss. "One day at a time is perfect."

She pulled his head back to hers and kissed him back, only her kiss packed a little more heat. He was totally on board with that and they spent long minutes kissing, learning one another's taste. The texture of lips, the feel of tongues, and the depths of mouths, exploring, tasting, discovering. It was a heady experience.

Jacqueline's phone beeped an alarm and she pulled out of his arms. "Time to re-apply sunscreen."

"Oh goody, let me help."

Jacqueline rolled her eyes at him but handed the sunscreen over.

CHAPTER FOURTEEN

Lake Chelan

Jacqueline had never in her whole life had sunscreen applied so meticulously. David quite happily applied the cream to every inch of her that wasn't covered, and a few inches that were. By the time he was finished letting his hands roam over her skin she was on fire, the man had heated her up, but good. Now if they just weren't out in the forest in the middle of the day, maybe they could do something about it.

He snapped the lid shut and handed the product back for her to put in her backpack.

"If I'd known you were going to make applying a little sun protection into a form of seduction, I'd have had you do it back in town where there was a bed nearby."

He grinned at her and winked. "I would be happy to apply anything you would like to your beautiful skin, when we have a bed nearby. But I doubt you'll need to worry about getting sunburned once we hit the sheets. At least not for several hours."

"Several hours?" she gasped.

He nodded very seriously. "Several hours. It's going to take me a long time to worship every inch of you. There will be no rushing, just a long slow buildup of extreme pleasure for both of us."

"Oh, my." She thought she might need to submerge herself in the stream to cool down, from the look in his eyes, and the words he was saying. They definitely evoked some powerful images.

They both turned to look at the water in absolute silence for a few moments.

Then she looked at him and he turned his head toward her. "So how long do we have to stay up here communing with nature?" she asked in a near whisper.

He looked at his arm as if there was a watch there.

There wasn't.

His chocolate brown eyes met her green ones.

"I think we've done enough communing with nature; shall we take this opportunity to return to town... and the B&B."

"My room or yours?"

He ran one finger down her arm, which sent shivers throughout her body. "You've got some of that lovely smelling lotion from Iris in yours. I could apply it, slowly and carefully, very slowly and very carefully."

"Done. Race you back to Betsy. Don't forget to bring the stuff."

She leaped up grabbed her shoes, sweater and backpack and went sprinting off toward her car, laughing, as he called out, that she was cheating.

She pulled her shoes back on as she waited for him to join her at the car. It didn't take him long; he'd pulled everything up inside the blanket and used it like a sack. His shoes were untied with no socks. He dropped his burden into the back seat and slid in all the way across the bench seat until he was right next to her.

Jacqueline turned toward him, and he captured her mouth in a hot demanding kiss. She fisted her hands in his hair and gave it right back to him, until they were both panting.

"While we get our second wind, drive! Don't hurt Betsy, but give her the gas, darlin'."

She laughed. "Betsy can handle it."

"Good, because I'm not sure how long *I* can handle it."

Jacqueline took off at a fast clip, he slid back to his side, and pulled on the seatbelt.

"I thought we weren't going to rush, that it was going to be a slow build up."

"Oh, it will be, but getting there to start with, needs to be quick."

She gave Betsy a bit more gas. "Sounds good to me."

"Whoa," he said as he gripped the chicken bar. "But don't kill us, because I will be very upset if we die in a fiery car crash before I get to relish your sweet body."

Laughing she took her foot off the gas a little, not too much, because she was ready for some action. She'd not had any in so long she couldn't even remember the last time. Clearly it had not been a memorable experience. She had a feeling this time with David, she would not be forgetting any time soon.

~

David loved hearing Jacqueline laugh in pure joy. Her whole being lit up and fun exuded from her. She was racing down the mountain, not too fast for conditions, and he'd been exaggerating, just a bit, about needing to hold on. It had made her laugh and that was exactly his plan.

He was certainly eager to get her naked, but giving her a fun time was the most important thing, especially if he was right and she had been on the receiving end of his father's attitude. The man did, in fact, think women were morons and nothing more than someone to fuck. He could be quite the ass, if he saw a woman that he decided was being uppity. So, David was going to do his best to help her forget all about her shitty lawyer.

Then once they'd gone their separate ways, whenever that might be—hopefully not too soon—he was going to do some digging and see just what it was his father was up to. The best part of his father's company was that they kept everything online, even the not so stellar stuff, so everyone in the firm could see what was going on, just in case.

But that was for later, now his job was to focus on the beauty next to him and give her the best time of her life, both in bed and out of it.

Her voice broke into his thoughts, "Straight, or right?"

He'd forgotten all about her need for directions. "Right."

He directed her to the B&B but before she parked, she said. "Um, do we need to go to the store first?"

He looked at her in confusion and her face turned a bright red. Oh, dumbass that he was, she was asking about condoms. "Nope, no need I picked us up some protection this morning, when I got the drinks."

"Oh, good. I didn't want to be indelicate, but…"

"No worries, my goddess. I have it all under control."

She raised her eyebrows. "Goddess?"

"Yep, you are in my book."

"Well then, let's go in, so you can worship at my feet."

"I intend to worship your feet, and your knees, and your thighs, and—"

She put her hands over her ears. "Enough. I don't need a play by play."

David laughed and pulled one hand down to kiss her fingertips, then looked up at her through his lashes. "Are you sure. It might be fun to describe in great detail."

"Actions speak louder than words, mister."

"Fine, let's action away." He pulled one finger into his mouth and gave it a lick.

She shuddered and yanked her hand away. "Well, I am going to go to my room and get comfortable while you bring in all this picnic crap. I don't want to attract bugs or rodents by you leaving food in the car. Goddesses do not like bugs and mice, and neither does Betsy."

He sighed as dramatically as he could and said, "Okaaaay, I will bow to your wishes, my goddess. But don't get too comfortable. I want to help with that part. It's a lot of the fun."

She shivered and he wasn't sure if it was deliberate or a reflection of her own thoughts on the matter. He hoped it was the later.

He gathered up all the crap they'd taken with them and left Betsy sparkling clean after quickly brushing out the grass and dirt that had been on the blanket. He put the food in the fridge and dumped the rest on the floor in his room, all except for the condoms. Those he took with him, ripping the box open as he went across the hall.

He found her resting on her side on the bed with a few of the buttons on her blouse undone, and he about swallowed his tongue. He wrenched his eyes away from the hint of cleavage showing, to take in the rest of her. The pose she'd picked set off her assets to the fullest and he wasn't sure he could move. Even her pretty bare feet enticed him. He didn't know where to start. She'd put on fresh lipstick, of bold red, and he wanted that color smeared across his whole body.

She gestured toward him with one finger to come closer

and he saw the bottle of lotion that Iris had made on the bedside table. He was also glad to see she'd pulled the comforter and sheets down, so they didn't ruin the pretty quilt on the bed. This was going to be a grand adventure for both of them.

CHAPTER FIFTEEN

Lake Chelan

Jacqueline was very gratified by the expression on David's face. He'd stopped dead right inside the door. His hands were filled with a box of condoms, he was attempting to open, but having very little success.

She wanted to laugh but didn't want to destroy the illusion of sexiness she'd tried to create. Apparently, it had worked because nothing was moving on him, except his eyes which were devouring her. Well, there was something behind his jeans that might also be moving, but it wasn't a voluntary action on his part. Still flattering to her, however.

But statue time was over, so she crooked her finger at him, and he finally managed to get his body to move. He dropped the mangled box of condoms on the bedside table and crawled up on the bed with her. She'd made sure there was plenty of room for him when she'd laid down in her seductive pose.

He croaked out, "My God, Jacqueline, you slay me. You are so beautiful my heart feels like it's going to burst from my body."

She gave him her Mona Lisa smile. "I think the challenge was, to be showing not telling."

"I can certainly use my mouth for better things than words. And those bright red lips of yours are where I want to start. I'm going to ruin your lipstick darlin', but never your mascara."

She couldn't help the giggle that escaped. She loved that song by Runaway June. "I've got plenty more lipstick, do your best."

David whispered in her ear. "Another time, I want you to use that mouth to smear that lipstick all over my body, but this time, I get to enjoy yours."

"That sounds like a great idea."

He threaded his hands through her raven hair and pulled her bright red mouth to his own, and ravished. Their tongues dueled and she wrapped her arms around his waist and pulled him closer, so they were plastered against each other.

∼

David could kiss her for hours. He pulled back so they could breathe, and she laughed at the lipstick smeared across his face. She grabbed a tissue and wiped his mouth. "I know you want my lipstick all over your body, but my white skin will suck that right up and it will look like I was in a fight with a hornet's nest."

He shook his head. "However, if I cover every inch of your lovely white skin with that delightful lotion, it won't be able to absorb color quite so easily. And I believe that was the first plan we had, back what seems like hours ago, but was only a few minutes. So, let's get back to plan A."

"I guess we got carried away and forgot the plan."

"I can't complain sweetheart, you have a very kissable mouth."

"Likewise, David."

He pulled back a little more and looked down at her. "Well the first thing we need to do, so I can slather you with lotion, is to remove some of these clothes."

She nodded sagely. "That would make things easier, I suppose."

He ran his fingers from the neck of her shirt down to the shadowy depths taunting him. "I see that you were feeling warm and started unbuttoning this pretty blouse, but I interrupted you before you could finish."

Her mouth lifted in a tiny smile that showed him she knew he was teasing her.

"So, I suppose it befalls me to help you remove it." He let his fingers caress her and then slipped the next button free. Pulling the sides of the shirt a bit wider he could see the tops of her breasts and wanted to kiss them, but the plan was lotion first, so he resisted the impulse and slipped the next two buttons free, which revealed the sexiest turquoise bra he'd ever seen.

The breath whooshed out of him and he couldn't move for a moment. He managed to swallow to get some lubricant in his totally dry throat and croaked out, "If I had known what was under this pretty blouse, I'm not sure we would have ever made it out of this inn, earlier."

She pulled him closer and whispered, "If you like that, you're going to love the rest of the matching set."

He couldn't breathe as his lungs stopped working, from the devilment in her eyes. She was going to kill him, he knew it. And she was enjoying every damn minute of it.

"Maybe we'll just work on the top half, until I have the strength for the bottom half."

Her laugh was pure wicked delight and it sizzled in his blood. Oh yeah, she was enjoying tormenting him… and so was he.

As soon as he got the shirt off, he was going to return the favor, although her soft, soft skin was going to do a number on him also. Oh well, the sacrifices one must make to give pleasure to a partner. And now he was just getting ridiculous in his own mind.

He finished unbuttoning the shirt and pulled it out from underneath her, to toss on the floor. He turned her onto her front so he could start on her back. Before he opened the lotion, he unsnapped her bra and then poured a generous amount of the creamy goodness on his hands.

The room filled with the fragrance as he rubbed his hands together to warm it up. He straddled her and then with long smooth strokes covered her back with the decadent ointment. Gently caressing her to work it into her skin.

He found a few tight muscles, so he added a bit more cream to his hands to knead the tension out of them. He knew he had accomplished his mission when she sighed and relaxed even more. He spent a few more minutes on her back and tight muscles, until he'd lulled her into complete relaxation.

Climbing off of her he gently and slowly turned her onto her back and straddled her again. Starting with her neck and shoulders he applied the ointment in long smooth strokes, checking to make sure there were no tight muscles. When he found her still fully relaxed, he used the cream on her arms and torso.

Finally, he removed the lace covering her breasts and his breath caught as he looked at her fully uncovered above the waist. She was gorgeous. He poured more of the lotion on his hands and began massaging it into her breasts. That got her attention, she opened her eyes and her breath stuttered.

"You almost put me to sleep," she muttered in a husky voice. "But now I am wide awake, that feels amazing."

He gave her a crooked smile. "I totally agree, it does feel amazing."

Her lips twisted into a smile that was dazzling. She didn't smile often, but when she did it was something to behold. He pinched her nipples just enough to get them to furl into tight buds. He hoped the lotion wouldn't kill him because he had to have a taste of those.

Before he could put his mouth where his hands were, she reached up and pulled his lips down to hers. The kiss was fiery hot. He'd clearly ramped her up with his massage. Not that he was complaining. She devoured his mouth, tongue, lips, and teeth, she practically inhaled him.

He was trying to give it right back to her, but she was nearly frantic. He. Loved. It. Even if he couldn't keep up.

Finally, when they both were going to pass out from lack of oxygen, she broke off the kiss and lay there panting. He took a couple of deep breaths and then put his mouth on those tight buds and she nearly leapt off the bed. Then she grabbed hold of his hair and held his mouth to her, like he was going somewhere, not hardly, he was going to enjoy that breast and then move on to the other one.

CHAPTER SIXTEEN

Lake Chelan

Jacqueline was nearly out of her mind with pleasure, she had extremely sensitive boobs and the man was sending lightning through her body with each caress and suckle. She wasn't sure she could stand the ecstasy. When he finally moved on to the second nipple, she knew it wasn't going to take her long before she had a massive orgasm. But she didn't want to come so quick, she was enjoying his ministrations, and her skin was loving the attention.

"David, you have to stop. I can't handle anymore."

He gave that nipple another large suckle and lifted his head to look her in the eyes, causing her breast to pop out of his mouth. "But I'm having fun and so are you."

"Yes, but, well, there is still the full lower half that's screaming for some of that lotion, and your expert application."

His eyes lit up like a kid seeing his first Fourth of July fireworks. "Yeah?"

She nodded. "Yes."

He moved off of her and unzipped her pants, then kissed the skin that was revealed. "Lift up a bit."

She did and he slid the pants out from underneath her, but before he'd fully divested her of them, he stopped and was entranced.

She smirked. "I told you that you were going to like them."

"Like is not nearly a strong enough word for what I'm feeling right now about that scrap of lace just barely covering you. Can I keep them and put them in a picture frame?"

She laughed and he shivered. "No, you can't keep them, they're a matching set."

"Oh, well I could keep both of them. I would buy you new ones."

"Don't be silly. Shall we proceed?"

"Oh yeah, I lost my train of thought, but I wasn't being silly. I was being dead serious."

Jacqueline rolled her eyes, as he kept muttering about not being silly, while he pulled her pants off her body and dropped them on the floor. Then when she was uncovered, he raked his hot glance over her from head to toe and grabbed the lotion.

He turned her over to lay on her stomach. "Back first, so I'm not tempted to stop half way, although that gorgeous booty of yours makes me want to bite it."

"Lotion, David, lotion."

"Yes, ma'am."

He dropped one little cold drop behind each knee which made her shiver, then he rubbed it in, and slowly proceeded down to her ankles and feet, massaging the muscles as he applied the cream. Her feet were singing when he was finished with them. Then he moved back to her knees and started working his way up. He spread her legs a little to give him full access to her thighs.

He pulled her panties down over her butt and then kissed one cheek. She shuddered at the feel of his mouth on her ass. It was amazingly erotic, that one little kiss. She continued to think about that little kiss as he spread the soothing lotion on her backside. When he was completely finished, he gave the other cheek one little kiss and she nearly melted into the bed.

This time when he turned her over, he slid her panties down and off. They were probably soaked anyway, so she was glad to be rid of them, except that left her completely naked while he was fully dressed. Somehow that was hotter than anything she'd ever experienced before.

David gave her a warm glance and said, "So lovely, you are so lovely."

Then he filled his hands again and set the container down. "I'm going to have to buy you more of that, we've used over half of the bottle."

"You can buy me more if you want, but I'm not complaining, and neither is my skin. It's been a wonderful use of the product."

He gave her a lopsided smile as he started at her feet. "It has been. But I don't think Iris needs to hear about how excellently we used it."

Jacqueline laughed. "If she's as shy as you said she was, then no we don't want to shock her. But you never know, sometimes those shy ones have hidden depths."

He guffawed out a sharp laugh. "You might be right about that. Maybe she made it for exactly this type of scenario."

"If she did, then kudos to her."

David was glad that Jacqueline had joked about Iris. His control had been ready to slip. He'd been holding on by a shred of willpower. The joking had helped cool his ardor somewhat and allowed him to continue his adoration of her body, most importantly the oh so soft, completely unblemished skin.

His goddess was amazingly beautiful, and her skin had loved the attention. He moved his strokes further and further up her legs getting closer and closer to the very core of her. He felt the tension growing in her body as his hands continued upward. It looked like they were both on the edge, not only him.

When he reached her most intimate area, he rubbed the lotion on her smooth skin, and she moaned and writhed. He couldn't help it, he had to have one small taste of her. So, he took it. Starting with an intimate kiss and then taking one small lick.

She gripped the sheets and held on as he gave her another longer firmer lick.

"Oh, my God, David. You have to stop. I'm going to come, and you're still dressed."

"Excellent, we'll work on number two when I get undressed."

He'd noticed her breasts were ultra-sensitive so when he suckled her, he lightly pinched her nipples at the same time, and she was off like a shot. Groaning out his name, as she came hard. He loved her responsiveness, she was so sensitive, and she didn't hold back.

Her skin dewed and turned a delightful shade of pink, she looked even more ravishing, and he was glad he had contributed to that.

He sat up on his knees and was enjoying the delectable sight laid out before him.

She opened one eye. "You're still dressed."

"Yeah, I've been having too much fun to take the time to disrobe."

"Now would be a good time, David."

He hopped off the bed. "As you wish." He dropped his clothes where he stood and noticed she'd opened both eyes to watch, and had even propped herself up on her arms for a better view.

"See anything you like?"

"Why, yes, yes I do. Several things in fact, and now it's my turn to touch."

"I'm not sure I can stand a lot of touching, I'm pretty close to the edge myself."

"Well, I suppose I can limit the touching, this time, but next time, it's my turn."

Next time, hot damn, she was already talking about next time. "We can do that."

"Good, now get over here, and let's see if we can open the box of condoms rather than just mangling it."

He chuckled and joined her on the bed after picking the box back up. She took it from his hands and had it opened and one foil packet out in seconds. She opened it with her teeth and looked pointedly at him. "Well get him over here, so I can help you get it on."

He wasn't sure he could stand her helping, but he supposed he didn't have a choice. He moved closer to her, so she could reach, and then about died from the pleasure, as she had a fun time rolling on the protection. She'd teased him mercilessly in that simple act. And he could tell by her expression, she'd known exactly what she was doing, and it had been very, very deliberate.

She laid back with a satisfied smile and spread her legs. He didn't have to have that action explained to him, so he moved into that open space and let his cock rest on her most sensitive area. He also used his chest hair to abrade her nipples and she flushed.

She reached down and took him in hand and guided him to her opening. He slid in and she sighed. "Much better."

David had to agree with that, but waited a moment to make sure she was feeling comfortable. When she wrapped her arms and legs around him and lifted her pelvis, he decided that was his cue to get moving. He could be obedient.

He started with long smooth strokes and she raised up to meet him and used her inner muscles to squeeze. The movement increased in speed and intensity as she urged him on with little mews of pleasure. The sound skittered through his blood and increased his drive to make her his, in every possible way.

He felt her nails dig into his back and assumed she was getting close again, so he rotated his hips a bit on the next few thrusts. Then he pulled back enough to lean down and nip at her breasts, that was exactly what she needed to send her soaring. She clenched down on him so tight, that it pulled him right along with her. They soared together above the earthly plane in a place reserved for lovers.

When they returned to earth, he rolled them onto their sides, their legs tangling together and dropped the condom in the trash. "That was amazing."

She stroked his damp hair back from his face. "I totally agree. What a wonderful vacation gift. Excellent stress relief and we have almost two more whole weeks to indulge."

He hoped that he could convince her to extend that, when they got back to Seattle, but now was not the time for that discussion. He jokingly said, "I might need to buy more condoms."

She looked over at the box of thirty-six he had purchased, and with a completely straight face said, "Yes, you probably will."

His eyebrows shot up. She just looked at him for a long time before he saw the tiniest smirk flit across her lips.

"You are both scaring me and teasing me, aren't you?"

The smirk got a little larger. "Maybe."

He rolled her over onto her back and straddled her. "Now you're going to get it." He started tickling her and she squirmed.

"Stop, David... Not fair... Naked tickling... Stop it... You big meany..."

She gasped when he finally stopped the tickle torture.

He still had her pinned beneath him, so he leaned down and licked her nipples, one then the other. Then she stopped breathing altogether.

"David."

"Yes, my love?"

"What are you doing?"

"Just enjoying these lovely bits of flesh." He pulled one nipple into his mouth and suckled.

She moaned, so he suckled just a little harder, adding a tiny bit of teeth to the mix. She grabbed him by the hair, and he didn't know if she was trying to stop him or hold him where he was. She was gripping his hair so hard, he hoped he didn't end up bald.

He moved to the other nipple and gave it the same attention.

CHAPTER SEVENTEEN

Jacqueline wasn't sure what to say or do. She'd never had a lover give her two orgasms and then keep going. In her experience, once a man had come to completion, they usually left, they might cuddle for a minute or two, but not long.

David appeared to be in no hurry to leave. Even if it was just to walk across the hall. She didn't know what to do about that. It made her feel awkward and uncertain. She didn't exactly want him to stop or leave, but she needed more information.

"David? Um, are you... well, are you going to stay longer?"

He looked up at her and frowned. "Do you want me to leave?

"No. Not really. It's just, I've never had relations with a man that stayed after the... um..."

His eyebrows shot up. "Are you telling me that every man you've been with got up and walked out after he'd gotten his release?"

She had no idea why he looked so surprised at that, which

only made her more confused and uncertain. "Well, yeah, they have. I've not been with a huge number, but the ones I have been with didn't hang around to chat or... um, whatever..."

David's frown got fiercer. "Well those other men were idiots, or maybe just self-centered bastards. I, on the other hand, enjoy being with you, naked or not, and I'm not in any hurry to leave. More sex or not."

"Um... okay." He didn't seem to think her past was quite normal. She thought back and asked herself if she'd wanted more from the others, and realized she'd never felt as comfortable with any of them as she was with David. She'd not known him very long and wondered why she felt so relaxed with him. There wasn't any particular thing she could point to, just a feeling of ease, and no need to prove herself. She'd been relaxed and happy when she met him, and he'd done nothing to change that.

"Unless you want me to leave. I don't want you to be uncomfortable."

She searched her feelings and could honestly say she'd like him to stay. "No, I don't really want you to leave. I mean I enjoy your company, too. It's just a different idea, but if you want to stay, then I'm good with that."

"Excellent, because I'm not in any hurry to leave, and I thought we might go to dinner later."

She loved that idea, he actually wanted to spend a lot of time with her and not just getting off. She felt the joy transform into a huge smile on her face. "That would be fun."

"Good."

He laid down beside her and pulled her into his arms, stroking her back as he chatted about the various places they could go eat. As he held her, she felt a warmth steal through her that she'd never experienced with a man before.

David was livid. How dare those other men treat this angel like a piece of ass. He had to work to keep his tone light and his body loose. Fortunately, all the harassment from his father and then his law school training held him in good stead, he could feel one thing and act completely opposite.

What he wanted to do was go pummel whoever had treated her so badly in the past, but what *she* needed was just someone to make her feel special and important. He was by-God going to make her feel like the wonderful woman she was, even if it killed him. He was pretty certain he would enjoy every minute of it, and it wouldn't even come close to killing him, but he was willing.

So, he held her close and talked about inconsequential things, while his brain tried to think of ways to show her how special she really was. He was going to take the next two weeks to demonstrate that those other men she'd been with were complete and total morons, while he treated her like the goddess and wonderful woman she was.

He noticed that Jacqueline relaxed as he held her. She'd been a little reserved and tense, even while having sex, but now she was wrapped around him and nearly boneless. David was glad he was the one to give her that peace, or confidence, or whatever it was. For being such a lovely woman, she didn't seem to have a lot of self-confidence where relationships were concerned.

She was perfectly confident about her work, other than the lawyer treating her like crap, but that served to indicate that she was strong and self-assured in that arena. But her hesitancy to be with him in the first place, and then her revelation about how men had treated her in the past, showed a completely different woman. Maybe he could help her with that, to become more assured in relationships. Although, if he was honest, he didn't want her with any other man. He liked her just where she was, in his arms.

CHAPTER EIGHTEEN

Lake Chelan

Jacqueline had never spent so much time with a man in her life, and she was having a wonderful time doing it. If anyone had told her she would be spending nearly twenty-four hours a day with some guy, she would have told them they had no concept of reality. But that was exactly what she had been doing.

After their picnic and first time together as lovers, they had been nearly inseparable. They spent the next two days at the amusement park and Jacqueline had been pleasantly surprised at what a great job they had done fashioning the park on the *Adventures with Tsilly* game. They had depicted all ten worlds, some of the areas changed with each new release, bringing in costumes and props that kept up with the variations in the game.

One of the main ones that differed was the post-apocalyptic adventure. It was housed in what looked like a huge bombed out warehouse, that part didn't vary, but inside they had followed the shifting story as the tale ventured further into the war-ravaged world, and new people were discovered.

Chris, whose brainchild the park was, had also taken them on a tour of the underground, or 'backstage'. It was fascinating to see how all the mundane workings of the park were hidden, so they didn't take away from the fantasy of being inside the game.

They had ridden on all the rides and had eaten in most of the areas, even splurging on some of the junk food. Many were high-classed items, without being too expensive. David was the one who had coaxed her into eating them. She wasn't a food snob and she ate her fair share of unhealthy food, but she tried not to do it too often.

David had insisted that a person could not go to an amusement park and not have some cotton candy or a waffle cone or something. She'd finally caved on the waffle cone; they had been freshly made and the butter pecan ice-cream had called her name.

"All right, David, if you will stop nagging, I will have a waffle cone with a scoop of butter pecan ice cream."

"Just one measly scoop? That will hardly fill the waffle cone." He shook his head sadly.

"Yes, one scoop, we just had a wonderful and filling lunch." The people coming out of the ice cream place had enormous scoops of ice cream on their waffle cones. She wasn't sure if she could even eat one scoop let alone two.

"That was at least two hours ago, and we've been walking ever since, burning off that lunch."

"Never-the-less. One scoop for me. You can have whatever you like."

He waggled his eyebrows at her. "I'm getting two, one of mocha almond fudge and one strawberry. I can pretend it's chocolate covered strawberries if I get a lick of both at the same time."

"You are a silly man."

When Jacqueline had finished her very large and totally

satisfying ice cream cone, David still had a significant portion of his left.

Jacqueline looked at his cone and then nudged him with her hip. "So, mister eyes-are-bigger-than-your-stomach how are you doing on that non-measly ice cream cone?"

"Hey, I didn't know they were going to give me half a gallon of each flavor."

She raised an eyebrow at him. "Did you miss seeing the people walking out of there with their huge scoops of ice cream?"

He shrugged. "I wasn't paying that much attention. Besides, I can handle it."

He took a huge bite and Jacqueline just shook her head. "Try not to make yourself sick, proving a point, that is unprovable."

He had another few bites and then groaned and tossed the rest in a handy trash can. "I hate to waste it, because it was delicious, but throwing it back up wouldn't be fun."

"Not really, no. So, I'm guessing the whirling bubble ride is not in the game plan for the immediate future."

He turned a little green and said, "How about that lazy river ride through America. That sounds more up to my current speed."

"I don't know if that's a good idea, last time we rode that I think you shocked a few children with your amorous activities." He'd had her in flames, and a family of four had frowned at them when they got off the ride.

"I promise to do nothing more than hold your hand."

She wasn't sure she believed him; he'd gotten the both of them riled up the last time they'd ridden it. "Mmmm, hmmm, I'll have to see that to believe it."

"I'm too full to do anything more, trust me on that."

She patted his belly. "You do seem to have a bit of a food baby."

"Yeah, and it's too full to even try to hide it. Let's go rest on the river ride."

She looked him over and wondered if they should call it a day. She never liked getting too full, it wasn't a fun feeling. "We don't have to stay. If you aren't up to it."

"No. I'll be fine in a few minutes. I just need to let some of that ice-cream settle. Maybe one of the stationary animals on the carousel would be good too."

"So, river ride first, carousel second and then we'll see how you're feeling."

"Sounds like a plan."

They'd spent the rest of the day there and had watched the fireworks over the lake. They didn't have a lot of them, especially with the Fourth of July coming up, but they had a few every night during the summer months. Tourists and the people on the lake loved them.

∾

David decided after two days at the park they could manage a day on the lake. Fred had texted him to say that the wreckage from the boat accident was all cleaned up. He'd also heard the family had been released to go home, fortunately they were Washington residents so didn't have far to travel.

He booked a daytime cruise with some water skiing and ordered them another picnic lunch from Amber. Fred had suggested an outfitter in town that would help with wetsuits. They'd gone and tried them on in the morning for the afternoon fun on the boat. Fred normally took fishermen out in the early morning and stayed until it started getting warm and the fish stopped biting.

The outfitter had taken one look at Jacqueline and had said he thought she was going to look great in a wetsuit.

David had glared at the man until he'd backed off. Jacqueline hadn't even noticed the man's lustful look, but David wanted to punch him. Twice. He couldn't remember ever feeling that way about another man checking out his date, he had to wonder about the violence of his feelings from this guy ogling Jacqueline.

After they were ready for the lake visit, they took their picnic lunch to *Tsilly's Rock*, Jacqueline had said she wanted to visit it, since all of the stories in the game started from that point, she wanted to see it in real life. It was just a large rock on the side of the lake, but Jacqueline insisted the place felt magical.

He didn't necessarily disagree with that idea, but he wasn't completely sold either. The fact that he was sitting on the rock having lunch with the lovely lady made it feel pretty magical, and that had nothing whatsoever to do with Tsilly, the *supposedly* magical lake monster.

It was a beautiful day to be on the water, the sky was a bright blue with a few wisps of clouds, which only served to emphasize how perfectly blue it was. It wasn't the muted color they often got in Seattle, where the denser clouds faded into a mist, that caused the sky to be nearly white with just a hint of blue. No, this was slap-you-in-the-face, get-your-attention blue. The lake—in contrast—was a darker color, it was a deep lake, so the color reflected that and was nearly violet in color.

Fred's boat was painted white with turquoise accents. Jacqueline loved the color turquoise, so she was enchanted and happily beamed at both men, which caused brain cells to fry. Fred managed to shake himself out of the stupor first.

"Alrighty, then, get yourselves settled and we'll be off. We'll start with some cruising of the lake and then get the toys out."

There was only one other couple on the boat, and they

were too busy with each other to even notice the rest of them.

Jacqueline whispered, "Why didn't they just stay at the hotel, or wherever? Why would they pay all this money to go on a boat ride and not even look around?"

David tore his gaze away from Jacqueline to look at the other couple. Since he'd had his eyes on her, rather than the lake, he didn't know what to say so he cleared his throat to give him a moment and muttered, "I have no idea."

She shrugged. "To each his own I guess, it just seems like a waste of money to me."

David had no room to talk, so he just turned toward the lake to point out interesting features and tell about excursions he'd had in some of the locations. He managed to keep her entertained with stories as they enjoyed cruising the lake on the beautiful summer day.

The water skiing was hysterical. David had never laughed so much in his life.

CHAPTER NINETEEN

Lake Chelan

*J*acqueline had been water skiing a time or two in Seattle, there were lakes everywhere, so half the population owned a boat. She'd never become adept at it, however. She either leaned too far forward and did a face plant or if she managed to lean back, her feet seemed to think they should each go in opposite directions of the other one and she ended up doing the splits. Today was no exception.

David would be next to her, expertly skiing, and then look over at her with a horrified expression.

"Lean back, like you're sitting in a chair," he yelled, right before she took a faceplant.

Then it was the other couple's turn and they managed to let go of each other long enough to also ski expertly, while David tried to give her tips.

The next time they went out, she got positioned leaning back just fine, and David grinned at her. But then her legs slowly started to slip apart.

David would yell, "Knees together."

Right before she splashed into the lake.

When they got back on-board David said, "So, you're not a great water skier."

Jacqueline sighed, "Actually I'm not a great any kind of skier. I'm just as bad on snow as I am on water."

"Why didn't you mention that? We didn't have to go on the water-skiing trip."

"I like going out on the boat, just not water skiing."

"I think he has a tube, too."

She shook her head and raised a hand like a stop sign. "No thanks, I get caught in those with my butt too low and my feet sticking up. It's not a pretty sight."

He was trying manfully not to laugh his ass off, and she could tell. She poked him in the stomach. "Go ahead and laugh. I've seen a video of me on skis and in a tube, and I laughed like a loon."

His mouth twitched. "I would never laugh at a lovely woman doing her best."

She said, "Well that's just silly. It's funny and I know it, so I give you permission."

"No, it's rude." A slight chuckle escaped.

"But funny."

"Maybe a little, you were trying so hard and your body just wouldn't cooperate." A little larger chuckle eked out.

"I was, but it seems to be futile for me." She gave him a sad and mischievous look.

David couldn't keep the laugh in. "Okay, you win, it was pretty hilarious."

She laughed right along with him. "Now, don't you feel better?"

"I do. You know that the boat trip I really wanted to take you on is the sunset cruise."

"Then why are we on this one?"

"I was easing you into the idea."

She rolled her eyes at him. "No easing needed. Sunset

would be better on my skin. I wouldn't have to look like a dumb ass on skis, and in case you hadn't noticed, we've already done the deed, so not much else that needs easing."

An odd expression flittered through his eyes, but it was there and gone before she could figure out what it was about. He said, "Well let's just enjoy the cruise from the boat and we'll sign up for a sunset cruise."

"Perfect."

∼

David knew he was going to need to tell Jacqueline the truth soon. He'd gotten online one afternoon when Sandy had asked Jacqueline over to run some ideas about the game by her, and damned if he hadn't been right. His father was indeed the misogynistic dick she'd been working with, some of the notes on the case had pissed him off but good.

The only good thing about the whole scenario, is that David had found out that his father had derailed the sentencing, only to run the billing hours up, to punish them for making him work with "those women". So, the good news was that it wasn't for nefarious reasons.

Which meant David had the chance to push his dad along and wrap it up. He'd put a couple of comments into the correspondence, to that effect, so he would have to see how far that got him.

He sure didn't want to tell Jacqueline that it was his own father that had driven her to the breaking point.

He also didn't want to tell her he was a lawyer. Or that he lived in Seattle.

She seemed to be so happy having a short-term summer fling. She'd mentioned it a few times, nothing specific, just how freeing it was that it had a termination point, so they didn't need to adapt anything, like working hours, eating habits, entertainment, and the like.

He knew those things were sometimes hard to compromise on, but not that difficult, especially when you found what appeared to be "the one".

David wanted to enjoy every minute of their *fling*, before he threw that monkey wrench into the works. He just didn't know if he let her assumptions ride for the two weeks, if she would rip him a new one when he told her the truth, preferably when he got in her car to ride back to Seattle. He'd flown in so didn't have any transportation of his own and could certainly cancel his return trip to spend the day with her on the drive back.

If she was still talking to him.

But he figured all was fair in love and war, so he hoped like hell she would laugh it off and be happy to see him when they returned to the "real world" in the same city, rather than half way across the state.

Jacqueline turned to him. "How are my face and neck looking? Are they turning pink? Do I need more sunscreen? The wet suit makes it easy for the rest of me."

He kissed her nose. "It's a little pink, and so are your cheeks. I see no other pinkness."

She whipped out her sunscreen and slathered it on, he helped her smooth it where she missed, and when they were done, kissed her nose again. He loved touching her soft porcelain skin and decided he could happily spread sunscreen on it for the rest of his life. And wasn't he getting way ahead of himself?

But now that the thought was out there in the universe there was no denying it was true. He just needed to convince the lady, and that was going to take some time to accomplish. He might not need to ease her into a sunset cruise, but forever was a whole different ball of wax.

They turned to look out over the lake and Jacqueline leaned up against him. He kissed the top of her head and sighed in contentment.

She whispered, "This is nice."

He couldn't agree more.

CHAPTER TWENTY

Lake Chelan

The morning of July Fourth dawned bright and sunny. She and David had given Betsy a thorough cleaning and she was gleaming and ready to go. They'd bought a few streamers to put on her once they got to at the parade's starting point. She'd heard the parade committee had little flags also.

Jacqueline was excited to put on her pinup girl costume, that she used for this specific holiday. Her blouse was sleeveless and bright red, with a big bow on the left side of her waist. The skirt was bright royal blue and she had some pretty red shoes she wore with the outfit. A big red bow for her hair and cat eye sunglasses rounded out the look.

She could hardly wait to see David's reaction. Dressing up occasionally to match Betsy was so much fun. People were often surprised by her normally formal manner, breaking out into the fifty's pinup girl world. Their reaction was always part of her fun in doing it. She'd had people stand and gape at her not knowing what to say, especially when she struck one of the signature poses.

David didn't know her as the strait-laced boss of a development team at a big-time game company however, he only knew her vacation girl self, so the pinup girl might not be quite as big of a shock for him.

He knocked on her door at the exact moment he was supposed to, the man was by far the most prompt person she had ever known. She arranged herself into the pose she'd picked out just for him and called out to come in.

When he walked in the door, she forgot all about trying to surprise him, because he looked amazing. The man cleaned up well. He had on a blue suit that fit him to perfection, a stark white shirt, and a bright red tie, she was afraid she might drool. He'd trimmed his beard and tamed his unruly hair. The man was sex on a stick.

After a flicker of hesitation when he saw her, David walked up, took her hand, and kissed it. "You look amazing and I want to kiss that bright red mouth, but I'll kiss your hand instead."

His lips lingered and he turned her hand over to nibble at the inside of her wrist. "And your wrist."

Jacqueline only shivered as he kissed up the inside of her arm to her elbow. Sparks were shooting throughout her body as he made love to her arm. The man had a very talented mouth. She was disappointed when he stopped and looked up at her through his lashes.

"I guess we better go, so we're not late. But can I start where I left off, later tonight?"

She was hot and bothered and didn't want to wait, but she'd made a commitment and needed to see it through. She gave him a hot look. "I'll be counting on it."

He grinned and pulled her hand through his arm. "Guess we better get the day started then."

Betsy was ready and waiting for them, they drove to the beginning of the parade route and got in line. David jumped out to put the red, white, and blue streamers on the car and

CONFLICT OF INTEREST

one of the parade helpers handed her the flags that easily attached.

Jacqueline didn't know who was going to be riding with them and didn't much care as long as it wasn't some jerk that people would be throwing rotten garbage at. Betsy would not be happy covered in filth.

When a high-school-aged young man and—what looked to Jacqueline—to be a coach appeared, she was relieved. Apparently, the kid had won some national award for track and his success had put their tiny high school on the map, so there was great enthusiasm for the boy and the coach, neither of whom quite knew how to respond.

Jacqueline noticed their awkwardness and whispered to the two, "Just be proud of your accomplishment and share the joy of that with the town. Smile and wave, give a thumbs up to your buddies and family. Have fun and smile, that's all you need to do, until you go off to college or the Olympics and then work your ass off."

The boy grinned and the coach relaxed. The boy nodded and said, "Yes ma'am, you sure do look pretty in that outfit. It matches the age of the car, doesn't it?"

"Thank you, and yes, it does. Now let's get in Betsy and we'll all act like we've been in many parades before."

The boy and the man folded their lanky limbs into the backseat, where she knew they had plenty of room, since she had the seat forward, and the older cars like Betsy had plenty of space in the back. David on the other hand might be more scrunched, but he'd never complained before.

The parade was surprisingly well-run, she was surprised at that, only because the town didn't have many parades and the one Sandy had helped with last year, had kept their whole team in stitches as Sandy related all the foibles that had occurred. She and Greg must have clued in the new people running this one.

The boy, Tom, and his coach, Kirk, did a great job and both of them were beaming by the end of the route. After they dropped them off at the end of the parade, along with the flags, they drove Betsy back to the B&B. They could walk back for the rest of the festivities, but she was going to change into some shorts and sneakers first. She guessed David might get more casual, too.

~

David took Jacqueline's hand as they set out for the festival on the lake. There would be fireworks later when it got dark, but now was an old-fashioned town picnic and music. The food and the music was being handled by the church. The sister of his reformed pyromaniac was an amazing fisherwoman, so between her fishing and Hank's cattle ranch, there was plenty of meat for the grills. Then everyone in town brought a side dish, Sandy had explained that there would be plenty of food so not to worry about contributing.

The same woman who was the fisherwoman was also an amazing drummer and her brother played bass guitar. They'd gotten some other musicians and had themselves a great little band. He was looking forward to the event.

David had been shocked to see that Tom O'Connor had been the one they were driving, he hadn't been around for much of the drama the family had gone through, but his mother had relayed the news. He was thrilled they'd pulled out of the difficult times and to see Tom as a town hero was thrilling, he'd been a pre-teen during the hard times.

He said, "You did a good job calming down Tom. He's from a good family, but they went through some difficult times a few years ago. Some of the attention he got back then wasn't positive, so I think he's leery of being in the public eye."

"If he's going to continue to be an amazing athlete, he'll need to get used to it. Besides, nearly everyone goes through tough times. How you deal with them, is what's important in the long run. It looks like he's done just fine."

"He has and so has the whole family, they really pulled together, and the town rallied around them, once they knew what was going on. His mom, Tammy, probably would have died if Chris hadn't found out what was happening. She was really sick and was trying to get better on her own. Chris called the doctor and it was found she had pneumonia, but she's fine now and is helping to run the art gallery, especially as the other women have more kids and less time to be there constantly."

"I don't think I met her. I talked to Mary Ann. She's a wild one."

He laughed at the description because it fit Mary Ann to a tee. "That she is. Tammy is older and more settled than Mary Ann."

"Is Tom her oldest?"

"No, Jeff is, he's away at college, getting a master's degree in something like rocket science. He's a smart kid."

Jacqueline nudged him with her hip. "Rocket science, huh? I wonder what it really is."

He grinned and looked confused. "I have no idea, but someone could probably tell you. It's a very small town."

The number of people at the picnic belayed the idea of it being a small town. There were people everywhere, and enough food to feed the state of Washington and part of Idaho, too. Of course, the whole town was there and the tourists and the seasonal people who came in to help in the summer, including a lot of college age kids.

He was surprised when a group of those young adults swarmed them.

A tall blond kid asked, "You're the lady with the Bel Air, aren't you?"

"That's such a cool car, how long have you had it?" A short dark-haired boy asked.

"Did you buy it restored? Did your boyfriend restore it for you?" A third person asked, looking at David.

Jacqueline held up her hands to forestall more questions. "Yes, I own the Bel Air. My father and I restored it together for nearly twenty years. Everything is classic on her, no modifications except those required by law, like seatbelts. Her name is Betsy and she'll be very glad to hear you enjoyed seeing her. She's got her own website where there are pictures of her renovations and lots more information."

David was surprised when she reached into her purse and then handed each of the boys a card with Betsy on it and a website. He felt a little left out that he didn't get a card but figured he could tease Jacqueline about that later.

When the boys had finally wandered off in search of food he said, "I didn't know Betsy had a website."

"Yeah, I put one together. Dad and I had taken lots of photos as we restored her and kept good notes. So, when she started gaining attention at events, I put together a website so fans could go look up all the information they wanted and see the progression of her renewal."

"Very smart of you. How many cards do you hand out to it?"

"Hundreds, and the page has had thousands of visitors, there is a guest book, but it's also got some counters to see where people click. There's even some merchandise people can buy, keychains, bottle openers, post cards, stuff like that."

"So, Betsy is big business?" he asked, surprised at all the work she'd put into a website for a car.

"Well, when I take her out, she can be. Interest wanes when she hasn't been out in a while. The website is pretty static now. It only changes if we go to a car show or something like that."

"Maybe you could put up an adventure log for Betsy, like her coming over here and her observations."

"That's a cute idea. I'll give it some thought." Her eyes glazed over as she thought about what he'd suggested.

He nudged her to get her focus back in the present. "Let's get some food, before it's all gone."

Jacqueline laughed. "I don't think you have anything to worry about in that regard. I think there's enough food to feed Washington and Idaho."

"No way, just all of us growing boys."

They loaded their plates until she thought they might collapse under the weight, and then found a spot to sit near Sandy and Greg.

"Hey boss. Betsy looked mighty spiffy in the parade," Sandy said.

"She did. The kid and the coach were fun to drive. They were a little nervous at first."

Greg said, "First time in the limelight. Not an easy place to be for some. You gonna stick around for the music and fireworks?"

David nodded. "Yeah, I want to hear Kent play."

"They do a good job with worship music on Sunday. They've played in the bar a few times. It should be interesting to see how they do outside."

"From the church to the bar. Sinners and saints in both places."

Greg waived a chicken wing at him. "You got that right."

Sandy and Jacqueline talked about work for a few minutes before he and Greg intervened. He said, "No work talk on a holiday."

Greg nodded. "Yeah, you two will get started and never stop."

Sandy rolled her eyes and said, "Fine. Come over tomorrow and we can talk, without male interference."

"I will."

"You guys need to come back into the bar before you leave. You've only got a few days left, don't you?"

David froze, but Jacqueline must have assumed Greg was talking to her when she said, "Yes. I need to leave on Saturday. The barge doesn't run on Sunday and I don't really want to take Betsy over the mountain."

Greg nodded, "That's a good call, she could probably make it since cars were built tougher back in the day, but no use testing that theory. So, come into the bar Friday night, and we can rock the place."

Before anyone could say anything more the band started up, and David thanked his lucky stars that Greg hadn't revealed his secret. They all sat back and listened to the music, that was played good and loud.

After their food had settled David told Jacqueline he was going to get them a plate of desserts to share. Greg followed him.

When they got to the dessert area, the music was not quite so loud. Greg said, "You haven't told Jacqueline that you live in Seattle, have you?"

"No, she thinks we're having a summer fling, with an expiration date. I'm not telling her until the last minute."

Greg shook his head. "That's gonna piss her off, you know. Women hate to be lied to."

"I'm not lying, I'm just not explaining the whole situation."

"Lying, and we both know it."

David didn't answer, he just filled his plate with a bit of all the desserts and then got two cups of the homemade ice cream.

As he walked back to Jacqueline, he saw his mom and made a quick detour to give her a kiss on the cheek.

"David, when are you going to bring that girl to meet me?"

"Soon, Mom." He wanted Jacqueline to meet his mother, but he didn't want her to spill the beans. He really needed to tell her the truth, dammit.

"Tomorrow will work just fine."

He shrugged. "Okay. I know she's planning on spending some time with Sandy during the day."

"Dinner time will be perfect."

She wasn't taking no for an answer. Maybe this was a hint from the universe that it was time to come clean. "All right, you win."

His mom looked thrilled. "Good, it will be fun."

David kissed his mom again as the band started on the next song, and walked back to Jacqueline wondering if he was blowing it by not telling her everything, as Greg had said. And now he needed to invite her to have dinner with his mother. It might be better to tell her, before his mom mentioned something, he didn't want her to.

CHAPTER TWENTY-ONE

Jacqueline noticed that David had gotten quiet and looked pensive after he went to get dessert. She wondered what had happened. He was still talking and eating the sweets, but something in his eyes was off. She wondered if it had to do with her, and was certain she didn't want to know, so she pretended she hadn't noticed and tried to draw him out of it.

Everything about the day had been perfect, so she didn't want to spoil it. She wanted to sit with his arms around her and watch the fireworks and pretend like this week was never going to end. She didn't want to go back to her job and the real world. She wanted to stay right here with David and coast through the days.

She refused to allow the real world to interfere until she had no choice. These last few days together were going to have to keep her going, maybe for years. Then the mayor got up, after the band was finished playing, to make some announcements. There were winners from the parade, for the various floats and marching groups.

Jacqueline was shocked to hear her name called out over

the loudspeaker for the best car in the parade. David got up and tugged her up to go get her ribbon. He grinned and kissed her forehead and pushed her toward the stage.

Betsy had won a few ribbons over the years, but never for simply driving a couple of people in a parade. Still it would look pretty on the bulletin board she kept for things like that. She accepted the award, waived out to the crowd, and went back to David.

"Congratulations, honey. She was the best car in the parade. Betsy deserves the recognition by the whole town not just those boys earlier."

Jacqueline shook her head at the extravagance of the award. "Thanks, it just seems a little over the top."

"Well some of the other car buffs might not agree with you. There seemed to be some competition that we didn't even know about." He nodded toward the side where a few of the other drivers looked back jealously.

"Oh, I had no idea."

"Neither did I. I'll bet your sexy outfit helped."

She laughed as she was meant to. "Not my fault they're all dumb boys, and I was the only pinup girl."

He pulled her into his arms and gave her a sound kiss, which helped her ignore the sore losers.

~

David had decided that Greg was right, and he needed to tell Jacqueline the whole story, but now in the middle of the town picnic, was not the right time or place. Maybe back at the B&B tonight would be the best time.

The idea made him both nervous and also excited. Maybe she would like the fact that they lived in the same town. He wasn't sure there was any way to make her like the fact that he was a lawyer, but the simple fact of the matter was, that he *was* an attorney, and he was good at being one. Now that he was working on more of the cases he wanted to and was also able to do some pro-bono work—for people like Kent—it made all the difference in the world.

He was a good lawyer and he worked on the side of the little people, that needed good representation. He was not a corporate attorney and that suited him just fine.

It was time for the fireworks to start, so he pulled Jacqueline in front of him and wrapped his arms around her, as the cool mountain air flowed down to the lake. It went from scorching hot to nearly chilly once the sun went down and the airflow changed. Being a city girl, she didn't know about this phenomenon and hadn't brought a sweater with her. So, he got to be the sweater, not a bad thing, in his mind.

He noticed Greg was doing the same with Sandy, who had lived here most of her life and did know how the temperatures dropped. Maybe it was more of a ploy to get wrapped up in each other before heading home. Sounded like a great idea to him.

They stood together watching the brilliant lights shooting over their heads, while everyone around them oohed and aahed. There were plenty of variety in color and action. He'd never seen the one where all the separate sparks turned into puffballs of tiny sparks, making him think of a full-blown dandelion. But his favorite was still the shower of golden sparkles, that reminded him of a weeping willow tree.

Jacqueline seemed to like the ones that whistled and shot off in all directions, and the ones that changed colors as each level exploded. The grand finale was spectacular as rocket after rocket shot up to fill the air with color and sound. They'd done an excellent job with choreography to the music that blared over the speakers. As the last spark faded everyone assembled, clapped, and shouted their approval.

When the show was over the lights in the park came back

up so everyone could gather up their chairs and blankets, left-over food, and families. David and Jacqueline helped Sandy and her mom tote the food back to the cars. Greg had gone to be with the fire department just in case there was any issues with the fireworks. There hadn't been any, but knowing Greg as they did, they weren't surprised to see him helping some of the older residents get to their transportation, even with the park lights up, it wasn't always easy to navigate the grounds, as night vision faded with age.

David and Jacqueline caught a ride back with Carol to the B&B, so they could also help unload, as Sandy waited for Greg.

Carol enthused, "What a fun night. I so enjoy not being in charge and just sitting back to enjoy the event."

David chuckled at the former mayor. "I saw you direct no less than five people and answer a lot more questions than that. You're still in charge, just from the back of the room."

Carol smiled. "All those years of experience come in handy, but I like the back of the room, now."

David nodded. "You put in your time at the front. Is it hard not seeing an Anderson at the helm of the city?"

"A little, not enough to take the job back, but... yeah, a little hard."

David said, "Maybe Sandy will take office someday down the line."

Jacqueline gasped. "Not too soon, I hope."

David patted her hand and Carol rushed to reassure Jacqueline. "I don't think we'll be prying Sandy away from her game any time soon, so don't worry about that. Besides, James is doing a fine job, there's no rush for him to move on."

∽

David was still acting a little odd when she dragged him into her room. "So, this morning you made some promises I hope you still plan to keep."

She held out her arm and pointed to the inside of her elbow. "I believe you stopped here."

His eyes heated and then he sighed. "I think we need to talk about some things first."

She put her hand over his mouth. "Oh no you don't, buster. I've been thinking about this all day and I don't want you using your mouth for anything more than kissing, and maybe licking, nibbling might be fine too. But no words, unless they are my name or 'yes, right there', 'don't stop'."

"But—"

"Nope, nothing you have to say cannot wait until tomorrow, tonight you have promises to deliver on."

He grinned at her and then said dramatically, "All right, if you insist."

"I do." She pointed to her arm again. "Start here."

"I could start over."

"No, you promised to start where you stopped, which is precisely here."

He took her arm and bent to kiss the spot, his warm breath caressed it and she shivered. But then he looked up. "Are you sure it wasn't a little lower?" He kissed an inch below the spot. "Or maybe it was a little higher?" His lips tickled the spot an inch above.

Her body was responding to his touches, tingles spread up her arm and then throughout her body. "No, I am quite certain, it was right here."

"Very well." He finally kissed the spot she had pointed to and she nearly lept out of her skin. He'd done a good job building anticipation.

Then he looked up again and she wanted to slap him. "My mom wants us to come to dinner, tomorrow night."

"If you don't stop stalling, you are going to be dead, then there will be no dinner at all for you."

He bent to kiss her arm again and then straightened. She was going to strangle him with her own two hands.

"But you'll go to dinner, right?"

She said through clenched teeth, "Yes, David, I will go to dinner, as long as you are still breathing."

He flashed her a grin and finally got with the program. She was nearly a ball of flame by the time he settled into the task. He more than made up for it, with long slow kisses on every inch of her body. He took his time, even though she tried to get him to move along a little faster.

She refused to admit it, but he knew exactly what her body loved, and he had every nerve ending sparking long before he joined with her. By the time he was done, she was completely worn out, and she was a very happy girl.

CHAPTER TWENTY-TWO

Lake Chelan

Jacqueline was starting to dread returning to the real world and Seattle, not only because she was going to have to deal with that jerk of a lawyer, but because she was going to miss David. She'd tried to keep reminding herself, and him, that this relationship had an end date. But the more time she spent with him, the less she liked that idea.

He'd gotten under her skin and she couldn't deny it, as much as she would like to, she'd always tried not to lie to herself. The fact was she really, really liked him. The days had been fun and the nights magical. They hadn't spent every minute together, but they had spent more time together than apart.

He'd invited her to come have dinner at his mother's house. That had freaked her out for a minute, but then she'd decided not to be a wuss and go have dinner with the woman. Now all she had to do was decide what to wear. She hadn't brought many clothes to dress up in, since her original plan had been to sit and read, and just hang out.

CONFLICT OF INTEREST

The two novels, she'd bought, barely had fifty pages read in them. But she wouldn't trade reading alone for spending time with the nicest, most considerate man, on the planet. And the nighttime fun was off the charts. So, she would pack up her novels and take them home to read when she was alone.

One of the things this vacation had taught her was that she worked too damn much. No one had ever expected it of her, and in fact, her boss had told her on multiple occasions, that some task or another could wait until the next day. But she'd almost always had done it that day, before she called it quits for the night, even if it meant working late on her laptop at home.

Jacqueline had checked in with her boss a time or two, and they were surviving just fine without her, which meant she really could slow down and take some time off on occasion. It was just her bad luck to have found a great guy on the other side of the state. She was determined not to get her heart broken when they split up and went their separate ways.

And she was stalling on getting ready. She did have one sundress with her, that she hadn't worn yet, so she supposed that was the one. She had just finished slipping on her shoes when David knocked on her door.

She called out to him and he peeked his head into the room. "Are you ready?"

She turned toward the door and he whistled. "You look amazing as always."

She smiled and curtsied. "Thanks."

He came into her room and drew her close. She pulled back and put her hand on his mouth. "No kissing, I don't want to have lipstick smeared everywhere, right before I meet your mother."

"Mom wouldn't care. In fact, we could call Mom and tell

her we aren't going to make it and stay right here and smear away."

"Oh no you don't, mister. I'm sure your poor mother has been cooking all day."

He grimaced at the truth of that statement and sighed. "I suppose that's true. So, can I have a rain check on lipstick smearing until later tonight?"

"I think that could be arranged. You do seem to like lipstick smearing."

He nodded like a happy puppy. "I do, I really do."

"Then it's something to look forward to, for later. Now let's go before you get sidetracked."

He sighed and tried to look sad, but she could see he was happy to have dinner with his mom, and to have her along with him.

They climbed into Betsy and Jacqueline wondered why he never offered to drive. Yes, she had a classic car and it was fun to go out in, but most men wanted to drive once in a while. He almost always paid for everything. She'd paid once when he'd gone to the men's room and the waitress had brought the check while he was gone. He hadn't made a fuss, but she could tell he was a little discomfited by the event.

Jacqueline didn't actually mind that he paid, because it made her feel special and he seemed to like doing it. But she probably made more money than he did, so she would like to pay once in a while, to make sure he wasn't going broke treating her all the time. But how to go about expressing that without stepping on his toes, she hadn't figured out. He had definitely been raised to be a gentleman, he opened doors and held chairs, and did all the other things that showed a woman respect, which included getting the check.

The only thing he didn't do was the driving, so she supposed she should be happy about that, rather than curious.

They pulled up in front of his mother's house, and she realized that she'd gotten cold feet on the short drive, now she wished she'd taken David up on his offer to stay at the hotel.

∼

David went around to the driver's door of Betsy and pulled it open. Jacqueline was staring straight ahead with her hands clamped to the steering wheel.

He crouched down in the door. "Hey darlin' what's the matter?"

She continued to stare straight ahead and whispered, "Cold feet."

"To meet my mom?" He laughed. "She's awesome, you'll love her, and she'll love you, too."

He didn't know what to think. He was the one that was terrified his mom would reveal his secrets, and Jacqueline would storm out leaving him to walk back to the B&B. He hadn't warned his mom, at all, so she could say anything. But he did want them to meet, they only had a few days left before they needed to head back to Seattle, so it was now or never.

"Come on, sweetheart, don't be shy. Mom is harmless." He hoped like hell he was telling the truth and that his mom wouldn't say anything he didn't want said. Not that he wanted her to lie, just not blab it all.

Jacqueline drew in a deep breath and exhaled slowly, then she turned to look at him, he gave her his best encouraging smile, which must have worked, even if it did feel like a grimace to him. She got out of the car, stood up straight, squared her shoulders, and started up the walk. He hurried to catch up to her and take her freezing cold hand in his.

His mom opened the door as they approached, and he

realized she'd probably seen them waffling in the street. She didn't let on, however, and she gifted them both with a bright smile, welcoming them into her house, which smelled heavenly. The homey smells immediately dispelled his worry and he noticed Jacqueline relaxed, too.

His mother didn't wait for introductions. "Oh, it's so nice to have you here, Jacqueline. You must call me Olivia, none of that misses stuff, David's father is an ass and I took my maiden name back the minute we were divorced. I understand you are Sandy's boss. Did you come to see the game's birthplace, too?"

Jacqueline gave his mother with a small smile. "I did, in fact. This little town has gotten quite famous."

"And just in time, too. People were leaving in droves. Not able to support themselves. Now we've got a booming little town. The construction company can barely keep up with demand. Your game company helped with that, by investing in the park, and all that advertising. It was a shot in the arm that's for sure. Oh my, here I am talking your ear off and you're barely even in the door. Come in, come in."

David and Jacqueline followed his mom into the living room where she had a platter of summer appetizers and both iced tea and lemonade. His mom had made some fruit skewers, a cheese and cracker plate, and a veggie tray.

"Jacqueline would you like tea or lemonade?"

"Lemonade would be lovely, thanks."

His mom waved at the appetizers. "Good, now have a few snacks, we'll eat in a little while. David what do you want?"

"I'll have tea, Mom. Thanks." Rather than waiting to be admonished he picked up a plate and handed one to Jacqueline, both of them took a fruit skewer and some other things to munch on.

His mother beamed at both of them and took a plate of her own. He knew his mom liked to fuss, but he wondered if she had a hidden motive, like maybe trying to get him married off. David had mentioned to his mom that he was spending a lot of time with Jacqueline, since he wasn't dropping by to see her as often as he would be if he wasn't entertaining the lovely Jacqueline.

David found he didn't mind the idea of his mom and a hidden motive, so he let it ride. He was not at all adverse to taking help where he could get it.

His mom babbled on asking all kinds of questions to keep Jacqueline engaged. The conversation was enjoyable to listen to and he loved the way the two women were interacting, like they'd known each other for years.

When his mom got up to get dinner ready, Jacqueline picked up the appetizer platter and he carried the pitchers of drinks in to set them on the table, then went back out to get their glasses.

Olivia fussed at them, saying that they were the guests, but they just ignored her.

His mom had made one of his favorite summer dishes. Slow cooked spicy barbeque flavored drumettes. It was a meal that was made in a crock pot, that he would swear was cooked on a barbeque grill. She served them with sticky rice and cucumber salad.

While they ate, they talked about the new movies that had come out recently and what was on the horizon. His mom was the movie buff in the family and even though she lived in a one movie at a time town, she'd seen more than both he and Jacqueline added together. So, she clued them in on what was good and what wasn't even worth renting.

When they had eaten nearly every scrap of food to be found, his mother asked, "Would you like to sit out on the porch and let dinner settle before we have dessert?

David groaned. "I don't think I can manage dessert, Mom."

"It's ice cream pie."

He looked at her and she grinned. "You knew that would get me didn't you, mother dearest?"

"Of course, I did. I am your mother."

Jacqueline looked between them. "What is ice cream pie?"

David shook his head. "How can anyone live as long as you have and not know what ice cream pie is? It's the most wonderful concoction in the whole wide world. Especially on hot summer days."

He stood and helped both women to their feet. Mom, you and Jacqueline go out and sit on the patio, while I put the dishes in the dishwasher."

His mother's eyes twinkled. "Sold. Come on Jacqueline, we'll take our drinks to the porch and let David work off some of his dinner."

―

Jacqueline followed her hostess out to the patio, where there was a very pretty view of the mountains. They sat on the lounge chairs with their feet up, and enjoyed the day starting to cool. "So, tell me what is this ice cream pie that David is so infatuated with."

Olivia laughed and glanced behind her. "Don't tell David, but it's one of the easiest things to make, ever. It's a gram cracker crust, either bought or hand made. Then the filling is plain, softened, vanilla ice cream and any flavor of gelatin, that is just starting to set, so it's cool but still liquid. You mix the ice cream and gelatin together, put it in the crust and then freeze the whole thing for two hours and garnish with whatever fruit the gelatin is. Raspberry is a favorite, but nearly all the other flavors are just as tasty."

Jacqueline was delighted that it was such a simple recipe, but David was crazy about it. She thought it was quite amusing that Olivia kept him from knowing the secret recipe. "That's so simple, but it does sound delicious. I suppose now that I think about it, I have heard of other types of ice cream pie, but yours does sound the best."

"The best part is it's refreshing and very light."

"It does sound delightful. Thank you so much for inviting me. I've had a wonderful time and now I'm looking forward to your special dessert."

"My son seems to be quite taken by you."

"The feeling is mutual. He's such a nice guy."

"So, is there a future for the two of you?"

Jacqueline shook her head sadly. "Unfortunately, not. I don't think our lives would mesh."

Olivia took her hand and looked into her eyes. "If there is a will, a way can be found. Don't give up a great man. There are way too many jerks out there. Believe me I learned that lesson the hard way."

"Your son is very caring, and I wouldn't mind spending more time with him, but I go back to Seattle and my very demanding job at the end of the week. I just don't see how we could work it out."

"I don't think it would be that hard, weekends maybe. But then again, I am prejudiced in thinking how wonderful my son is, and that it would behoove you both, to give your relationship a bit more time."

Jacqueline just nodded. She wondered if it really was possible. Could they take turns visiting each other, or maybe both of them start out and meet for a weekend rendezvous in Leavenworth? She would give it some more thought.

David came out of the door with the drink pitchers, asking if anyone wanted a refill. Jacqueline looked at him with a new perspective. What if she did make the effort? And if he also was willing to work at it?

She held out her glass to mask the confusion and speculation, he was very observant, and she didn't want him getting any ideas, until she'd weighed the suggestion in her mind. He topped off her drink which was nearly full, but he didn't mention it.

He set the pitchers down on the table and pulled up another chair, there were only two loungers, so he put his feet on Jacqueline's chair. "Not quite ready for pie, but I did peek at it and it looks delicious."

Olivia said, "I should have had you put it in the fridge to soften a bit. You two stay out here and enjoy the evening while I do that. I'll be right back."

When she had scurried off David raised an eyebrow. "So, you two seemed kind of pensive when I came out. Anything wrong?"

She wasn't about to tell him what they had been discussing, not until she had time to think it over. "No nothing at all, but she did tell me the secret ice cream pie recipe."

"She did? That's not fair. I've been trying to get it out of her for years."

"Maybe she just wanted to keep it a secret to get you to come over."

David rubbed his chin. "Could be."

CHAPTER TWENTY-THREE

Lake Chelan

Jacqueline had begged off an outing with David this morning. They'd stayed up late into the night, making love with an intensity that had confused her. She needed some time away from the man to think through how she felt about him, and what his mother had said. She decided to walk while she pondered.

She didn't disagree with his mom, but she'd never really set her sights on getting married. She had a rewarding career. She had friends. She could have a date anytime she wanted. But she also knew that both going out with friends and dating a man were pretty far down on her priority list.

It wasn't that she didn't enjoy herself when she went out, but after a long day or week at work she wanted to simply hang out at her house in comfortable clothes and not go anywhere at all. Watching a movie or something on TV was relaxing, while going out with people was not.

She also usually fell asleep earlier than being out on the town would allow her to do. So, she'd never gotten in the habit of having a night life all the time. She had to admit she had enjoyed her dates with David, but they were not having them after coming home from a long day at the office. Would she enjoy him after a full day? She had to admit, that she might, as long as they didn't have to go out all the time. But so far David had been pretty chill, she thought he might be happy to sit on the couch and chat, as opposed to going out into the bright lights of the city.

She was definitely going to miss the man, which was why she was out walking. What might be an acceptable way to mesh their lives was something she wanted to think about. She couldn't see herself spending every weekend away from home. She still needed to do laundry and relax on the weekends. Maybe a couple of times a month they could get together. It was only a two-hour drive to Leavenworth, they could meet there, halfway between the two locations.

Or would it be better to just let it go and die a natural death when they separated. That idea didn't feel good right now, but might actually be the better thing for the long run. Just make the end quick and painful, but not for long.

She looked up and she realized she'd walked to *Tsilly's Rock*, she laughed and wondered if Tsilly had answers for her. She didn't believe in what Sandy's game supported, that Tsilly did exist and was a magical being, that could take her on adventures or answer questions.

She sat in the shade of the rock and stretched her legs out, part of the rock almost hung over the lake so sitting where she was, she could just barely get her feet wet. She pulled off her sandals and slid her feet into the cool lake water. Here at the shallow shoreline the sun heated the water enough not to be freezing.

She leaned her head back against the rock and muttered, "What do you think Tsilly? Should I cut it off sharp and quick or figure out a way to get together occasionally?" She leaned her head back against the rock, closed her eyes and let her mind drift.

CONFLICT OF INTEREST

She didn't know how long she sat there with her feet in the water and her mind drifting along, thinking about David and all the fun she had when another voice said clearly, "Don't let anger rule over your heart."

Jacqueline opened her eyes and looked around, no one was near. She decided she'd fallen asleep and had dreamt the voice. Unless it was Tsilly answering her, a wry smile curved her lips at that thought. Imagining the lake monster speaking to her.

She said, "Was that you Tsilly?" She knew she was being silly, but it was kind of fun talking to a mythical creature.

The voice returned and this time she realized it wasn't spoken aloud but rather was in her head. "Don't let anger rule over your heart."

"What's that supposed to mean? Anger at who?"

This time the voice in her head said, "Trust your heart, not your head."

Okay, this was getting weird. Maybe she was getting sunstroke. She started to stand to get back to the house when the voice spoke again. "Love is worth the trouble. Trust your heart, don't let anger rule."

Jacqueline finally said, "All right, message received. Um, thanks."

She stood and realized she wasn't alone anymore. Standing on top of *Tsilly's Rock* was the town peacock in full array. The sight of the bird, both startled and amazed her, how did she not hear it arrive? What had Sandy said about the peacock?

Jacqueline thought back to conversations with Sandy. It was something about the peacock showing up to give his stamp of approval on whatever was going on. Many times it was marriage proposals, but there had also been other times, like the opening of the amusement park, where the peacock had flown up to the top of the carousel and displayed his plumage. And the parade that Sandy and Greg had put on, the peacock had picked one of the cars, and had ridden on the hood during the entire parade. The parade started off the fundraiser for the helicopter flights to the hospital in Chelan, for people needing more than their town doctor and his little clinic could manage.

So, what was it doing here? It certainly didn't know what she'd thought she heard Tsilly saying. That was just a foolish idea. Of course, thinking Tsilly was talking to her was even more foolish. She must have sunstroke; it was the only rational answer.

She distinctly heard a laugh and Tsilly say, "Rational is for sissies." Then the peacock ruffled his feathers and cawed. Double whammy.

∽

David's cell rang and he looked at the number. His mom. "Hi, Mom. We had fun over there last night."

His mother didn't even say hello. "David, have you told her the truth yet?"

"What truth?"

"The truth that you live in Seattle and are a lawyer. She probably won't hold that against you, but she might the lying."

"I'm not lying, Mom. Just not explaining everything."

"Lying, David. Don't blow it. She's a great woman for you."

He sighed, his mother was right, she was perfect for him. "I was going to tell her the night of the fireworks, but, well, she had other ideas."

"Fine, but you've only got a few more days. Don't blow it, Son."

CONFLICT OF INTEREST

Before he could answer, the phone went dead. He said into the void, "Bye, Mom."

David knew he really did need to tell Jacqueline. He wanted to spend time with her in Seattle, he knew his heart was already set on driving back with her, rather than taking the flight he'd planned on. He simply didn't know how to broach the subject. He'd been out wandering around town thinking about it.

He'd gone by the art gallery to ask Mary Ann which quilts Jacqueline had liked. He thought maybe he would buy one for her, since she'd had trouble making up her mind. Mary Ann said she'd come in yesterday and bought one. Shaking her head, Mary Ann had told him that Jacqueline had dithered for a long time trying to decide between the two and had eventually used eeny-meeny to pick one. He paid for the second one and asked Mary Ann to mail it, and a necklace and earrings set he thought she would like, to his home in the city.

He looked up ahead and saw Jacqueline hurrying along the sidewalk. He jogged over to catch up with her.

"Hey beautiful, what's your hurry."

Jacqueline looked up at him with an odd expression, then she masked it. "I just thought it was time for me to get out of the sun."

"Have you had lunch? I was thinking of grabbing something at Amber's, or Greg's if you want fried foods and a darker room. Or there is also the pizza place or—"

"Enough choices! Let's go to Amber's, that salad bar is amazing."

David nodded, "Excellent choice for this hot day."

David decided if the place wasn't packed, and they managed to snag a private table where no one would overhear their conversation, then he would tell her he lived in Seattle and see how that went. The lawyer part could wait a few more days, it wasn't likely she would find out anytime soon.

David walked in to find Amber seated at the lunch counter and very few people in the room. He hadn't realized how late it had gotten, but they'd obviously missed the lunch rush. Amber looked up, when the bell jingled, she waved to the restaurant. "Have a seat anywhere you like, Kimberly will be out with water and menus in a moment."

David grabbed a couple of menus off the hostess stand and waived them at Amber. "Water is enough for now, no hurry. We're mostly here for the salad bar, but we'll take a look."

Amber nodded her agreement, so he led Jacqueline to an empty corner not far from the salad bar. It looked like they had recently restocked it after the lunch rush for the late customers like themselves.

Jacqueline sat and eyed the cold buffet. "I didn't realize it had gotten so late. I am kind of famished."

"Do you want to look at the menu? Or are you set on the rabbit food?"

"The salad extravaganza is calling my name."

He chuckled and gestured toward it. "No need to wait then, go ahead and get some salad. What do you want to drink?"

Jacqueline didn't hesitate to take his advice. "Iced tea would be great, unless they have an Arnold Palmer, that's my favorite."

David laughed. "I'm sure they can manage to pour a glass half full of lemonade and the other half with tea."

As Jacqueline hurried toward the salad bar, he used looking over the menu as an excuse not to join her. He decided fate had put into his lap the exact time to talk to the woman and tell her the truth. He just hoped she didn't throw her salad at him when he told her.

Now all he needed to figure out was the best approach. Time to do some quick thinking, counselor. David was going to use the very training she deplored to figure out the best way to tell her his news. God help him.

He wasn't sure he would be able to eat much so he decided the buffet would be the best bet. He gave Kimberly their drink orders and stood to join his goddess at the salad bar. Hopefully, she didn't have a Greek goddess's personality —or power—because he might end up as a frog if she did.

CHAPTER TWENTY-FOUR

Lake Chelan

Jacqueline was hungry, but part of her was also flustered at David appearing right after she left the lake and the peacock and Tsilly. She was in a state of turmoil and didn't want him to notice, even though he was most of the cause of the turmoil. Maybe especially because he was the cause.

When he joined her, she looked at her plate and realized she had enough salad on it for three people. Good grief, she was nearly a basket case. David glanced at her plate and one eyebrow rose, but he had the good grace not to say a word, she was grateful for that.

She poured on some dressing and went back to the table, hopefully she could make a dent in the food, so it didn't go to waste. She hated wasting anything, but for some reason wasting food really set her off. Maybe she could get a doggy bag and apologize profusely. Or pay for a second salad.

She needed to get a grip and not act like an idiot, David was eventually going to notice the state she was in and she really, really didn't want to explain. It would make her sound like a crazy person. It sounded crazy to her, and she'd been there.

When David sat, he had just a small salad on his plate, she found that odd, well maybe he could share some of hers. Maybe he'd thought of that when he'd seen her plate piled high.

He looked at her with an intensity she'd not seen before. "I need to tell you something."

She dropped her heavily laden fork to her plate as dread roared through her. He looked so solemn.

David ran a hand around the back of his neck, and then put his clenched fist on the table, a moment before placing it in his lap. "I haven't been exactly honest with you."

She just looked at him with what she hoped was a blank expression. What was he going to say? Was he married? Deathly ill?

"I let you believe I lived here. I don't. I live in Seattle."

She blinked and waited for him to continue, but he didn't, he just sat there waiting for her reaction. "You live in Seattle? But your mom lives here. So, you really are on vacation, just like me."

"I am. I needed a break from my job, so I came to visit my mom." She noticed him look away for a second and wondered what he was leaving out.

Jacqueline didn't know how to feel. He'd kind of lied to her, or at least let her believe he lived here, and she should be pissed about that. But she was too happy that he lived near her to force an anger she didn't feel. Is this what Tsilly had been alluding to?

"That's all? You're not married or have cancer or something?"

"No, what gave you that impression?"

"You were just so somber; I expected a bigger confession."

He looked aside again but shook his head and smiled.

"No, I just didn't want you to be angry that I let you believe I lived here."

"I never really asked. I assumed based on the fact your mom lived here and you grew up here."

"I lived with my dad in Seattle part of the time after my parents divorced."

Jacqueline wasn't at all surprised by that, many children spent part of the year with one parent and part with the other.

David asked, "So, would you be interested in pursuing a relationship back in Seattle?"

Jacqueline was more than willing to do so, but she tempered her answer, so that he didn't think withholding the truth from her was a good plan for the future. "I might consider that. I do work long hours at my job, however, so we won't be living in each other's pocket there, like we have been here."

David finally relaxed and a genuine warmth filled his eyes. "I work long hours, too. I'm sure we can work something out."

"So, do you really live in Seattle, or one of the other cities?"

"I live in Sammamish, actually."

Perfect, not far away at all. Jacqueline gave him a happy smile. "I live in Issaquah."

"Heck, we're practically neighbors. I've got an excellent barbeque grill and I know how to use it."

"Sold." She picked up her fork and took the large bite of salad that had been waiting for the conversation to end.

He stabbed his fork into her salad, too. "You can't possibly eat all that and I was too nervous to put much food on my plate. I'll help you."

"You're right, I can't eat it all. I was distracted and piled way too much on my plate." She was thankful his mouth was full so he couldn't ask what had distracted her. Something had just occurred to her and she hoped it would keep him sidetracked long enough to forget about her distraction.

"So, you've not had a car this whole time, did you leave it in Chelan?"

"No. I flew into Wenatchee and took a shuttle to Chelan." He tapped his fork on his plate in a nervous sort of way. "I was wondering, if maybe you would enjoy some company on the drive back to Seattle. I could cancel my flight."

That surprised her, although Sandy had suggested the same thing for her own arrival. The idea of driving back with him sounded wonderful. "I think that might be fun, to drive back together."

"Excellent, I'll cancel my flight."

They spent the rest of the meal talking about driving back. Where to stop and what she might want to see along the way. He'd driven it so many times over the years that he gave her lots of ideas and told her stories about some of the more memorable drives.

∼

David was relieved that his news had been received so easily. He'd been tempted to tell her the whole story but had decided one issue at a time was better. He was looking forward to riding back with her. He'd done the drive so many times that he was bored by it. But it would be a whole other story with her by his side. If they had the time it would be fun to spend a night in Leavenworth, she might want to get back as soon as possible, but he might as well ask.

"You're booked on the barge for Saturday, because it doesn't run on Sunday. Do you need to get back right away?"

"I was going to drive straight back to do laundry and get

ready for next week." She paused and he could see her thinking about it. "What did you have in mind?"

"I was wondering if you wanted to stop in Leavenworth and wander around, listen to the bands they have on the weekends and look at the street fair. Then maybe spend the night there and head out in the morning. It would make for two shorter days of driving rather than one long one."

"I think that sounds like fun. I would probably not do it if it were just me, but the two of us would make it memorable. The laundry can wait. I didn't bring my work clothes with me so washing these can be done a few days later."

"Great. I'll book us a room." He pulled out his phone and a few clicks later it was done. One more day with the lovely Jacqueline before the real world intruded.

"I take it you had somewhere in mind."

"I did, I've heard good reviews on the place and I've always wanted to try it, but like you, when I'm driving between Chelan and Seattle I usually blast right straight through, with maybe a stop for lunch in Leavenworth."

Jacqueline said, "I've always wondered about taking the snow train in the winter to see it all dressed up for Christmas."

"I have too. Let's do it!"

She laughed. "Seriously? What if we aren't together anymore?"

"Well I don't plan to break up with you, and it's less than six months away. I hope we're together a lot longer than that. I've got many more ideas to try out." He waggled his eyebrows at her to take the seriousness out of the declaration. He didn't want to scare her with what he was thinking. What he'd been thinking for several days, if not from the first moment.

Her skin turned a delightful shade of pink. "All right, we

can look and see what tickets are still available, I hear they sell out quickly."

"The key dates yes, but I'm sure there is something we can find."

"Since we don't have a release of the game this year, I shouldn't have any trouble getting away. The years we have a new version come out it's pandemonium until the very last day before Christmas. It's an all hands-on deck kind of thing, with promotions and advertising and whatever else pops it's little head up."

She shook her head. "I hope there's no more sabotage. That pretty much ruined Christmas two years ago. With us shuffling everything to try to find the porn."

"Porn? In a children's game?" He knew there had been sabotage but his father had glossed over what the sabotage was.

"Oh, yes. It was awful. It didn't show up in debug mode. In fact, it had to be run on a non-linked system to even get to it. And it was a series of events that triggered it, in several dozen places. If one of the engineers hadn't been a fanatic about making sure it ran perfectly on stand-alone consoles, we might not have found it in time to prevent shipment."

"That's atrocious. I can't imagine the backlash that would have happened if some little kid had found it."

"Right? We'd already burned thousands of copies for people to buy in the stores and thousands more with the code to download it. It was about five minutes from being shipped when he found it. And it wasn't simple porn either, like naked women, no it was a more deviant variety that no little kid should be exposed to."

"That sounds like a disaster of major proportions. How did you find the culprits?"

"Sandy actually figured it out from the actions of one of the teachers here in Chedwick. He'd been certain we had pulled the game and were working on something new. Since he'd been part of the original game concept, he was wanting in on whatever new thing we were doing."

"Ahh, that makes sense."

"Since we weren't doing anything new, he kept pestering Sandy and eventually stole her laptop. Since the sabotage, we'd gotten very paranoid and set up tracing programs and a fake profile on all the laptops. So, they caught him red-handed in minutes, in the fake profile."

"But…"

"He wasn't the saboteur, but his brother worked at the company that had sent the hacker to ruin us."

David was shocked at the story and even more appalled at his damn father stalling and dragging out the end, to this nasty business. Putting pornography in a children's game was the lowest of lows in his opinion. He decided right there that the first thing he did when he got back to Seattle would be to confront his father and let the other partners know the full story. He was livid and this was the last straw, his father was an ass and he was done with him.

He didn't want Jacqueline to sense his ire, so he stuffed it down and made appropriate comments of horror at the situation, proclaiming that this year would make up for her yucky Christmas before. Hot chocolate and a cozy trip over the mountains into Leavenworth, to enjoy the season would be just the ticket for her to forget the Christmas catastrophe. He was certain he could make some arrangements that would be fun. He would start to work on that, once they got back.

CHAPTER TWENTY-FIVE

Lake Chelan

Jacqueline and David spent Friday in the mountains, hiking and picnicking, then after a shower and change of clothes joined the town at Greg's bar. It was a rowdy experience as the whole town seemed to take the night off to play. There was a live band and lots of dancing, many people at the pool table, and a wild tournament at the dart board.

She looked around at all the activity, the sound, the people, the laughter, the food, and the drinks. It was like an oasis, in this sleepy town, of vibrant activity. She saw Mary Ann, from the art gallery, dancing up a storm, she seemed to be dancing with another couple. Jacqueline thought she recognized the woman as the one who owned the bakery, she'd never seen the guy before. She knew Mary Ann was married, so she wondered where her husband was, but then remembered that he was a hotshot firefighter and since it was the middle of the summer, he was probably out at some wildfire somewhere.

Jacqueline didn't think she'd like being married to a guy that wasn't around three to six months every summer, but she figured that's how they had met so it was something Mary Ann expected. Probably still not easy. But if you loved the guy, his career came with him.

When they got further into the controlled chaos, she saw Sandy at a table near the bar. Sandy caught their attention and beckoned them over to join her.

"Hi guys, I was hoping you would make it," Sandy shouted above the din.

Jacqueline sat and shouted back, "You tricked me."

Sandy held up her hands in surrender. "I did not. How did I trick you?"

"You knew David lived in Seattle."

Sandy grinned. "Oh that, yes I did. I thought you two might be great together and if you knew he was from Seattle you would bolt. So, I just didn't mention he lived in the Puget Sound area."

"I wouldn't bolt, just because I knew he lived in the Seattle Metro. What makes you think that?"

"Because you always do, you work too hard and you need some good stress relief." Sandy yelled back.

"You think David should be stress relief?" Jacqueline yelled back just as the song ended.

The silence in the bar was deafening, as every head swiveled in her direction. *Oh God just kill me now.* She wanted to hide under the table.

David grinned and spoke loudly into the silence. "I'm happy to be your stress relief, darlin', any time, any place."

Several other guys shouted out, "Me too."

David slid his arm around her waist and said. "Sorry boys, the goddess is all mine."

Everyone laughed and the band started up a new song. She sagged against David, her face still burning in embarrassment. Sandy patted her hand in sympathy, but there was a light in her eyes that belayed the act.

David whispered in her ear. "We're leaving tomorrow and by the time we get back here no one will remember."

That perked her up since she didn't plan to come back, maybe ever. She turned a smile on him and felt her face start to cool. Then he whispered in her ear, "I can't wait to be your stress relief in Seattle."

Her face heated right back up, fortunately a waitress came to take their order. She ordered the largest frozen margarita they had. She didn't normally drink them, but she wanted the ice and the tequila. Maybe she could get drunk and forget all about the man that was both confusing and relentless. One minute he was soothing her, the next he was torturing her, he kept her off balance, there was no two ways about that.

When the waitress left and Sandy was distracted, she elbowed him and whispered fiercely, "Stop that."

He simply laughed and waggled his eyebrows, causing her face to heat once more as she envisioned what he might have in mind. The man was a menace.

∽

David was enjoying Jacqueline's blushes. He loved that he had the ability to brighten her cheeks with just a look. He was also pretty damn glad he had been given the ability to stake his claim in front of the whole town. He'd seen some of the other men checking her out and he hadn't liked it. Not one bit. So, when the opportunity to defend her and let the others know she was with him had arisen, he'd grabbed it with both hands.

And being her stress relief? Oh yeah, sign him up.

He still had to tell her about being a lawyer, but that could wait, maybe she wouldn't realize it for a long, long time. Maybe even after the sting of working with dear old dad had worn off. That would be the best of the best. His father was such an ass to women, unless he was trying to get in their pants, and then he was all smooth and charming.

His mom had all but forced him into counseling, he thanked his lucky stars he'd managed to avoid becoming more and more like his father, he was so damn glad. The counselor had given him the tools, to see when he was spiraling down into those same behaviors he despised in his father. He wanted to rejoice in the freedom, and how better to do that than dance with his own personal Aphrodite.

David leaned over and spoke in Jacqueline's ear, "Want to dance, lovely lady?"

She took another big drink of the margarita she was sucking down like it was water and nodded. He was happy to notice when she stood, she wasn't drunk or even tipsy. He figured if they danced a while and then ordered some food, he could keep her that way. He wasn't a jerk about drinking, but he didn't want to carry her back to the B&B either.

A hang-over in the morning before driving for a couple of hours straight, wouldn't be fun. He could do the driving if needed, but he didn't know if she liked other people driving her car. He would simply be proactive and keep her busy. He supposed that some of the drinking might be to alleviate her embarrassment, so maybe he should back off on that, too.

The first song was fast and happy, and they both danced with abandon. Nothing subtle or smooth about it. Flailing arms and legs were the order of the day, and they were not—by any means—the only ones. It was lucky that people didn't end up bruised and broken from all the thrashing about on that dance floor.

They were both laughing and exhausted by the time the song was over, so when the band started up a slow ballad, he was more than ready to pull Jacqueline into his arms.

She muttered, "I'm kind of sweaty."

David grinned. "Sweetheart, we all are, after that. But we'll be sweaty with fashion and flair."

She looked up at him through her lashes, humor lighting her eyes. "I suppose that's true. All right then let's dance with fashion and flair, and some sweat on the side."

He laughed and spun her in a circle, which caused her to hold on tighter. Excellent.

Too soon, the ballad was over, and the band started up a line dance.

He asked Jacqueline, "Do you know how to do this dance?"

"No, and I don't want to try. Let's go back to our table and order some grease-laden fried food."

David shook his head and chuckled, but they did as she suggested. Chicken fingers, fries and deep-fried veggies were the choices they made. Her margarita was all watery—now that the ice had melted—so she pushed it away and ordered her normal selection.

Greg came over with some food for Sandy and himself and they chatted with the married couple while they ate. He'd never seen Greg look so content than he did with Sandy by his side. When Greg got up to go back to work, he said to Jacqueline, "It was nice to meet you Jacqueline, I hope you'll come back again."

Jacqueline said, "I did enjoy it, but I haven't taken many vacations, the game company keeps me busy."

Sandy laughed at her boss. "Yeah you've taken exactly one vacation in the whole time I've worked for you. This one right here, right now."

"Guilty."

Greg raised an eyebrow and tried to look menacing. "I'll know who to hunt down if Sandy is working too hard then."

Sandy looked at David. "Maybe you can slow her down."

He shrugged. "I can try."

Greg slapped him on the back. "And you, don't be such a stranger."

David shook his head sadly. "I can try. Might have better luck with Jacqueline."

Sandy looked at him in mock horror. "Oh, that's not a good sign at all."

Greg pointed at him. "You could always walk away like I did."

And didn't that sound like heaven, but David was determined to at least try to fix some things. It went against his nature to just cut and run. "It may come to that someday, but that day isn't today."

"I understand, well good luck to you both and come back soon." Then he walked off to spell the rest of his employees, so they could get off their feet for a few minutes and refuel.

David watched Greg walk away and felt a sense of satisfaction flow through him. He was glad he'd spoken to Greg and had cleared the air. They may never be best friends, but the enmity was gone and that was a most excellent outcome. Now that he was onto his father and his tactics, David could keep the tension between Greg and himself from coming back. He might need to buy his therapist flowers.

Sandy pulled out her phone and looked at it. "I think I'm going to head home. David, it was great to see you. Jacqueline, I'll talk to you on Monday. Have a safe drive over the mountains and tell Betsy I said bye. Maybe give her a nice fender rub."

Jacqueline laughed. "Will do. Have a good night and I'll see you Monday on Skype."

Before David could even ask Jacqueline what she wanted to do, Mary Ann bounced over and took Sandy's seat. "So, you're leaving tomorrow. That's sad. I didn't get to see you nearly as much as I had hoped." Mary Ann looked at him and frowned. "I suppose David has been monopolizing your time."

Jacqueline's face turned a bit pinker. He didn't think anyone else would notice in the dim lighting, but he knew every inch of her delectable body and could see the slight color in her cheeks. He didn't mind her blushing on account of him and his monopolizing her.

His goddess said, "We have been rather busy. There is a lot more to do in this little town than I expected."

Mary Ann grinned. "Isn't that awesome! We were dying out just a few years ago and now look at us. Going strong. Makes a person think anything is possible."

David snorted. "Sure, anything is possible with the right idea, stellar financial backing, and a thousand people working hard to make it possible."

His statement didn't slow Mary Ann one bit, she nodded happily. "Exactly. Isn't it wonderful?"

He wasn't sure he could take much more of little miss sunshine and optimism. He stood and said, "I'm going to get a refill, do you ladies want anything?"

Jacqueline shook her head. "I've had enough alcohol. A glass of water would be nice."

Mary Ann parroted, "Me, too."

By the time he got back from using the men's room and getting their drinks, Mary Ann and Jacqueline were out on the dance floor tearing it up. He was perfectly happy to sit back and watch the show.

CHAPTER TWENTY-SIX

Lake Chelan

Jacqueline tried to force her eyes open, if they got moving early enough, she and David could load Betsy on the barge on its way uplake then ride along and see the sights. But if she didn't get her exhausted ass out of bed, they would have to load Betsy when the barge was on its way back to Chelan. They'd never found the time for the ferry trip, so this was her last chance to see the rest of the lake.

Mary Ann had kept them out last night much later than they had planned. She couldn't figure out how the woman managed to go, go, go, all the time. It was like she was a human Energizer bunny. She was a mother of a one year old, for goodness sake, and for all practical purposes—this time of year—a single mother.

When Jacqueline had questioned her on staying out so late, she'd just laughed and said she didn't get out much in the evening, and she was taking full advantage of Trey's mother being in town and wanting some alone time with little Nicole. She'd laughed at herself and said she'd left skid marks on the way out the door.

Jacqueline had enjoyed her time hanging out with David's friends and dancing with Mary Ann. She was glad they had done it, but the result was that she was dead tired. Now all she had to decide was did she want another couple of hours sleep and miss the lake ride or go see the sights tired. She could smell coffee and breakfast calling to her, but she didn't think she had the energy to get out of the comfy warm bed and drag herself downstairs.

She wasn't sure exactly where David was, after they'd finally left the bar, when Greg had basically pushed Mary Ann out the door and told her to go home to see her baby, she and David had come back to the house and enjoyed the horizontal tango before falling dead asleep.

She knew he'd told her where he was going when he got up, but she couldn't remember and wasn't sure she'd been completely awake. She started to roll over and then stopped when every muscle on her body screamed in protest. For all the working out and staying in shape she did, dancing with Mary Ann had used muscles she didn't even know she had.

Jacqueline chuckled, thinking if she lived here, simply having Mary Ann as a friend would keep her in better shape than her outrageously expensive gym membership.

David walked in about that same time, his hands laden with a breakfast tray and coffee. She held out a hand beseechingly for the elixir of wakefulness.

"I only have two hands, so you'll either have to get up, or wait until I set the tray down," he said with a smile.

"Can't get up. Mary Ann killed me. Lifting one hand is all I can manage."

"Gonna be hard to drive Betsy from the bed."

"The elixir of wakefulness will cure me."

"Elixir of wakefulness? Well alrighty then. Here you go madam, a nice large mug of healing."

Jacqueline managed to sit up enough to take a long drink,

glad it wasn't boiling hot. Then she set the mug on the bedside table and flopped back into the bed.

David laughed at her. "Dramatic much? So, are you going to get that beautiful body out of bed so we can take the boat trip, or are we going to take our sweet time, and join them on the way back? I'm sure I could think of something to keep us occupied for a little while."

"Oh no you don't, you are part of the reason I'm tired and sore! If we stay here longer there will be no more shenanigans, only sleep." She shook her finger at him and then slumped back into the pillow.

David rubbed his chin and then shook his head sadly. "Nope, I don't think that's possible."

Jacqueline opened one eye and peered at him, the devilish grin and the glint in his eyes told the story of where his mind was going. Although she knew she would enjoy every minute, she also knew it would make her more tired and maybe even more sore. She should probably get out of bed and away from temptation and the sexy man.

She sat up enough to take another long drink of coffee and watched David over the top of the cup. Decisions, decisions. She decided the elixir of wakefulness was doing its job well enough that she could get up, and she really did want to see the rest of the lake.

"No more hanky panky for you, let's get Betsy to the barge. I want to see the rest of the lake."

David tried to look sad, but it wasn't quite convincing, she decided he wanted to get moving, too. He sighed dramatically. "If we must."

"Are you packed?"

"Yes. Is there anything I can do to help? Scrub your back, for instance?"

"No, the only thing you can do is get out of my room."

He sighed again even more dramatically.

She decided the only way she could get ready in time was to give him a chore. "Actually, how about you go get Betsy filled up with gas, so we don't have to stop in Chelan."

"But we should eat breakfast first, don't you think? Fuel ourselves and then Betsy."

She'd forgotten all about eating, but he was right, they should eat. Now she sighed dramatically. "I suppose you're right; food is a necessary evil."

He lifted the lid off one of the plates and a delicious aroma wafted toward her. "With these yummy offerings from Carol's kitchen it won't be too evil."

Her mouth was salivating from the smell. "You might be right about that. Let's eat."

He grinned and handed her a plate to load up with goodies.

After they'd chowed down about half of it, he asked, "Did you get everything from the art gallery that you wanted?"

"Wanted, no. Decided to buy, yes. If I bought everything I wanted, I'd have to take out a second mortgage on my home or get a roommate."

David laughed and then slid her a sly look. "I could rent out my place and be your roommate."

She thought about that idea as she chewed her food. He'd been easy to be with here in Chedwick, but living in her house in Seattle? She had no idea how that would be. She swallowed and said, "Let's table that idea for now. We've only known each other two weeks."

He winked at her. "I can be patient."

She wondered what exactly he meant by that. He didn't really know her well enough to move in, that was just silly. He didn't wait for her to answer but stood and started gathering up their breakfast debris. She snagged her purse and took out her keys and two twenties.

He took the keys and pushed the money back into her

hand. "I'll buy the gas. You just get your pretty self dressed and packed, and we'll get on our way."

She didn't think it was right he should buy the gas, but she'd discovered in the two weeks she'd known him that he wouldn't take her money if he didn't want to, so she gave up and put it in her purse.

"I'll give you forty-five minutes and then I'll be back. If you're ready, we leave, if you're not, you'll need another shower." He kissed her on the forehead and walked out the door, the look in his eye when he'd said that made her shiver.

Jacqueline realized, after he'd left, that he was the first human to drive her car, besides her dad, herself, and an occasional mechanic. Clearly, she trusted him. But not enough to challenge him with his last statement. She leaped up and started packing, everything but what she planned to wear on the trip home and her toiletries.

∼

David was surprised as heck that she'd handed him the keys to her baby. She didn't even know if he had a license or if he drove like shit. He didn't, he was a good driver, but she didn't know that. She trusted him with Betsy, but not her home.

He chuckled, he wasn't really planning to move in with her, at least he didn't think he was, but she'd looked startled at the idea. He'd been pretty surprised when the words came out of his own mouth, he'd been teasing, mostly. Maybe testing the waters, a bit.

She'd not denied the possibility forever, just for right now. Which suited him just fine, after all, she didn't know he was a lawyer, or the son of the jerk lawyer she'd been dealing with. Until those two things were revealed he couldn't think about moving this relationship forward.

The idea of taking things to the next level might be the

only incentive to telling her the truth. It would be the only thing worth revealing the damning secrets. He needed to hustle now, he wanted to go by and say farewell to Kent, get some road trip snacks and drinks, check in at the art gallery, fuel up the car and get everything loaded. And he had only forty-five minutes.

He set the breakfast tray down in the kitchen and kissed Carol on the cheek. "Delicious. We're going to head out in about an hour, thanks so much for having us."

"I'm glad you enjoyed yourself and Jacqueline."

He let out a quick guffaw. "Yeah, didn't see that coming, but I'm glad it did. Keep your fingers crossed for us, will you?"

"Better than that. I'll offer up a prayer or two."

"Excellent. Well I'm off to get ready for the road trip." He shook the keys at her.

Carol's eyebrows rose nearly to her hairline. "She gave you the keys… to Betsy?"

He nodded with a shit-eating grin covering his face.

"Well, you may not need those prayers, then."

"Nope, you promised and I'm holding you to them."

"I'll keep the bridal suite open."

He barked out another laugh. "Might be a little early for that, but we'll keep the idea in mind."

Carol just gave him a Mona Lisa like smile, and he hurried out the door.

He got gas and filled half the back seat with snacks and drinks. Then he debated on whether to see Kent first or Mary Ann. Kent was probably the safest. So, he drove to the glass shop at Nolan's house. Kent hadn't started blowing glass yet, but he was gathering his supplies to do so, when David walked into the heat.

Kent put down what he was carrying and came over to shake David's hand.

"I didn't get your sculpture quite finished."

"That's fine. Do I get to see it before I go?"

"No, until I get it finished it will look weird and dirty. I'll finish it up and mail it to you in a week or two, if that's okay."

David was surprised Kent didn't want to show him what he was working on, but didn't argue, artists were a strange bunch of people. "That's fine. Here's my address."

After he'd scribbled his address on a handy piece of paper, he pulled his wallet out of his back pocket and Kent frowned. "You just put that away. This is my gift to you for getting me off the hook and into this incredible situation."

"Are you sure about that? I don't expect you to—"

"Absolutely, you helped me out when you didn't have to, and didn't charge us. This is my way of thanking you."

"You are already thanking me by proving my faith in you was not in vain. You thank me every day that you don't set fires."

Kent ducked his head. "Thanks, my life is so much better than it's ever been."

David slapped the young man on the back. "Glad to hear it. I'll see you next time I'm in town."

Kent grinned. "I'll look forward to that."

David felt ten feet tall, helping that kid to a better road was the best feeling in the world. So much better than how he felt after speaking with most of his other clients. He really didn't like a lot of the clients his father's law firm attracted.

Maybe it was time for a change. He might just look into that when he got back home. Certainly, there were many options where he could work and feel good about it at the end of the day. He had no idea where to start, he'd allowed his father to groom him for his law firm. David had never considered taking another path. But after talking to Kent and listening to all the trouble his father had put Jacqueline through, he was beginning to think he wasn't long for this world of cut-throat, manipulative legal work.

Was he really thinking about changing law firms? Yeah, he was, and the idea made him feel better than he had in a long, long time. Maybe he would find the freedom and happiness Kent had found.

He decided to run by his mom's house for one last hug from the woman who had kept him sane, and not totally perverted by his father. He looked at his phone and decided he had time if he didn't dawdle.

When he charged in the door to his mother's house, he startled her.

"Oh David, you scared me. What are you doing here? I thought you were leaving today."

"I am Mom, but I just wanted to give you one last hug before we left. Thanks for being my anchor in the storm of my father."

"You're welcome. You look happier than you have in a while. Is it Jacqueline?"

"Partially Jacqueline, yes. But I'm also going to start looking around at other law firms."

His mother's eyes filled with tears and she sat on the closest surface. "Oh, David. Are you sure? Your father won't be happy about that, but I've hoped and prayed you would someday get out from under his thumb."

"Yeah, I know he won't like it, but I'm not like him. I want to help people. People like Kent and Jacqueline. I don't want to live my life trying to screw everyone to make more money and have more prestige. That's just not me, regardless of how hard Dad tried to make me that way."

"No, you've always had a kind soul. I hope you'll find a perfect fit, both in your job and in your life."

"Thanks Mom. I'm thinking a lot about both of those."

"Jacqueline is a very sweet girl; you could do worse."

He hugged his mom and kissed her on the cheek. "I'll keep you in the loop."

"You do that."

He hurried to the art gallery, only to find out it was Mary Ann's day off, which he probably should have been able to figure out based on them staying out all night last night. He decided he could call her and get the same information once he was home. He just wanted a few more hints on the kinds of things Jacqueline liked, Mary Ann could send him screen shots, and even ship things.

So, all his errands were done, and he had five whole minutes to spare, so he bought more of the lotion and soap Jacqueline had purchased earlier and sauntered out to the car.

CHAPTER TWENTY-SEVEN

Lake Chelan

Jacqueline managed to get packed, showered, dressed and even some make up on, in the forty-five minutes David had given her. She felt quite proud of herself and went down to chat with Carol while she waited for David. She would let him haul her suitcase down the stairs, the same as he had when she'd first arrived.

She thought back to that first day and how she'd made a fool of herself in front of him. What a difference fourteen days made. She wasn't sure she was in love with him, but she was certainly something. She didn't want their time together to end. She enjoyed being with him too much for that.

But love? She just didn't know. Jacqueline wasn't sure she would actually know love if it rose up and bit her in the ass. But maybe that was the nature of the beast, quiet but deadly.

She'd thought about the idea of him living in her house the whole time she'd been packing and getting ready to leave. Other than the idea of it, she'd realized that it really didn't sound bad at all. Jacqueline didn't think he'd been serious, just joking, but it was still out there in the universe to think about.

So, think about it she did.

When she found Carol in the laundry room, Jacqueline was more than ready to put those thoughts aside.

"Carol, thank you so much for having us in your home. This has been the most relaxing enjoyable time I've ever had in my life. At least since I graduated from college and started working."

Carol gave her a warm smile. "I'm so glad to hear that. I hope you come back again soon."

"I will definitely keep that idea in mind."

"Maybe you and David will come back again. Christmas is very lovely here, you know."

"Oh, well David did mention taking the snow train into Leavenworth."

Carol nodded. "Leavenworth is lovely that time of year also. Do you have family in Seattle?"

"No. I'm an only child and my parents were much older when they had me, so they are gone now."

"In that case you should definitely come back for Christmas, David's mother would be thrilled to have him here for the holidays. Most of the time he spends it in Seattle, but he would be happier coming here with you."

Jacqueline could feel a blush steal over her cheeks. "Oh, I don't know about that."

"Don't know about what?" a male voice said from behind her. David.

Carol said, "Coming back here for Christmas."

David scrubbed a hand around his neck. "We'll give it some thought, but now we better get on our way. Are you all packed up?"

"Yes, the suitcase is upstairs."

"Be right back."

Carol said, "Just remember what I said, you would be very

welcome to come back at Christmas. With or without David. But I have a feeling about you two."

Jacqueline wasn't touching that with a ten-foot pole, so with flaming cheeks, she gave Carol a hug and went out the door to see if anything in the car needed rearranging. She was shocked to find half the backseat filled with snacks and drinks and other random purchases. David had been busy while she packed and showered.

She remembered the trunk was filled with the picture that someone named Rachel had taken. Mary Ann had said she used to live in Chelan but had recently moved to Colorado to marry a cowboy. She and her best friend Alyssa had both moved there, causing quite a stir in town. She didn't know much about that, but the picture had been lovely and would look great in her living room, or bedroom. It was gorgeous, but it was also large, she probably should have mailed it.

David came out the door and carried her suitcase to the car rather than using the wheels.

"It has wheels."

"Yeah but they don't work down stairs, and sidewalks can be touch and go. It's just easier to carry."

"For you, maybe."

He touched her nose with one finger. "Exactly why I am bringing it and not you."

"I don't think it will fit."

"Ah, ye of little faith. Stand aside and watch a master."

She watched as he deftly arranged the suitcases and her other purchases to make a nice flat shelf for her picture to sit neatly on top. Which freed up the rest of the back seat, she noticed the snacks and drinks were left behind. It wasn't that long of a drive, so why did he need a ton of snacks? Men were weird.

His suitcase was tiny compared to hers, but she figured that was normal. Guys didn't carry a ton of extra stuff with them. Especially shoes.

∼

David was trying to stay busy and useful, hoping that Carol had not been matchmaking with Jacqueline as she'd done with him. He'd known Carol all his life and could take her meddling with a grain of salt. Jacqueline hadn't known her long and he hoped she hadn't made Jacqueline uncomfortable.

He didn't want the woman running scared. She hadn't really given him much of a clue as to how she really felt about the two of them. They'd talked a little about barbequing and a few other shared interests, but that's as far as it had gone, other than his one remark about being her roommate. He probably should have kept his mouth shut about that. There was nothing he could change now, but lay low and let things progress, he just hoped she wouldn't drop him off, never to be seen again.

Even if that was his future, he had one more day with his goddess and he was going to make the most of it. Starting with a slow ride on the barge up to Stehekin. Stehekin was much smaller than Chedwick, there were only a couple hundred people who lived in the area and a lot of those people lived further up the river in remote areas. They were beautiful places but not easy to get to.

The handful of families that lived near the landing ran the tiny gift shop and restaurant where the ferry passengers could eat. There was a magnificent bakery and some cabins where tourists could stay for a few days, that was a little further from the landing. A ranch, with some nice accommodations and great food, had some riding trails if people wanted to borrow horses. The only other modes of transportation were bicycles, little rangers that held up to six people and were basically a modified golf cart, and a red shuttle bus that drove a route up to high bridge and back.

He and Jacqueline wouldn't have much time there, just a few minutes while they unloaded the supplies the barge was delivering. Which meant they wouldn't see much, but maybe someday he could bring her back for a longer visit.

If everyone hadn't scared her off. Including him.

He hoped today was not the beginning of the end of their story. He wanted her in his life for a long time. Maybe it could be the end of their beginning and they could spend the rest of their lives together. He was only a little surprised that that didn't scare him to think about. He was clearly getting more comfortable with the idea.

He sighed internally, and got out of Betsy, now that they were loaded on the barge. Jacqueline joined him and took his hand to stand by the side and watch the water flow beneath them. The day was bright and the little nip in the air was tolerable. He decided he could use the coolness as a great excuse to put his arms around her, to block the breeze and keep her warm.

She didn't seem to mind that idea at all, in fact she leaned back into his embrace as the barge started its slow journey towards the top of the lake. He was content and decided he could stand there and hold her all day.

Jacqueline sighed. "This is nice. So peaceful and the views are gorgeous. I've never seen a lake that is such a dark blue color."

"It is nice. I think the color is because it's so deep. But I don't really know for sure." He didn't mention that the best part of this whole thing was holding her next to him. He'd been on this journey a few times in his life and it had always been enjoyable, but with her wrapped in his arms, enjoyable took on a whole other meaning.

Jacqueline snuggled back a little closer, her backside against his front. She sighed, then said, "I'm not looking forward to going back to work. This has been such a wonderful vacation. The idea of going back to all that stress is not a happy thought."

"Yeah, I know what you mean. Maybe we can sneak away on weekends and capture a bit of peace. Mount Rainier has some great places to get away. Or Leavenworth, or one of the islands. It would be fun to explore those places with you."

"Hmm, the idea does have its merits, but if we spent all our weekends away, we would run out of food and clothes, and our houses would get all dirty and nasty."

He chuckled. "Well maybe we could get away every other weekend then. Get all of our errands and household chores done one weekend, and then play the next."

"We can give it a shot."

With those six words, David felt hope soar, that Jacqueline was thinking along the same lines of spending more time together. He squeezed her tight. "We can be thinking about our first adventure. Maybe Bainbridge island."

"Oh! I love Bainbridge, but I've only gone on day trips over there, spending a night might be fun."

He wanted to find some remote cabin with a great view of the water, where they could relax and de-stress from their jobs. Touring around the island would not take long, it was pretty small. They could have their meals at the few restaurants and maybe do some walking. "I'll look into lodging and see what's available in two weeks."

"Okay. I'll pencil it into my calendar."

"Pencil? How about a sharpie instead, so it's permanent?"

Jacqueline laughed and turned her head so she could see

him. "That's exactly what I told Sandy when I called to see if they had an opening."

He kissed the top of her head. "Great minds and all that."

She snuggled back into his arms and they both sighed in contentment. He'd just secured another two weeks with her. He could offer to barbeque and maybe grab some takeout a couple of times. He'd have to see where she lived, to decide if he could help her out here and there around the house.

He'd also have to check his schedule with the ambulance, and get it on an every other week rotation. They might wonder about the change in availability, but when it came right down to it, Jacqueline was going to be a priority in his life, as long as she would let him be by her side.

When they got to Stehekin, the barge operator said they would have a half hour or so to enjoy the area, and that he would blow the horn when it was time to leave.

Jacqueline looked at the two buildings at the landing and whispered, "Do you think we can find something to do for half an hour?"

David grinned at her. "The gift shop has some fun things." Then he tugged her along after him.

By the time they'd shopped, gotten a drink at the restaurant, and used the facilities, it was time to return to the barge. Just as they started toward it, the horn sounded. They took up their spot and were ready for the return, downlake to Chelan. The ferry had radioed and been told they didn't need to stop by Lucerne or back at Chedwick, so the next stop was Chelan.

David said, "You bought more of that lotion."

"I did. I wanted some more and it's good to help the local economy. I don't know how those people survive year-round; they can't have a lot of tourists in the winter."

"No probably not, but they've been there for a long time, so they've figured it out."

He decided he would hold onto the set of lotion and soap he bought, for a while, maybe it could be a Christmas present, if she hadn't kicked him to the curb. If she did plan to get rid of him, he'd use it as a parting gift. A Christmas present would be much better.

CHAPTER TWENTY-EIGHT

Lake Chelan

The drive to Leavenworth was more fun with company. It wasn't a particularly pretty drive, but as David kept up a happy banter the miles flew past. They stopped here and there to see the sights, or buy some produce, at little stands in the towns they passed.

She was surprised when they did partake of his snacks and drinks. They planned to eat in Leavenworth, but with the barge trip it would be a little past lunch time when they got there, so the snacks did come in handy. She supposed he had more knowledge of the return drive than she did, since he'd done it many times over the years switching between parents.

As they neared the town, they debated what to eat.

David said, "So there are several places that serve German food like brats and beer. There are a couple of all-around American food, a pizza place or two, and a diner with hamburgers and malts, a place Betsy would feel at home in. Plus, a whole slew of other places. Pretty much anything you might want to eat."

"I have been thinking about brats and beer since we first started talking about stopping there for the night."

"All right well there are many to choose from. From a basement cellar that is always packed, to an outdoor beer garden, to a really nice place with a view of the Cascades, it has all kinds of food not just brats."

"I like the idea of the cellar, maybe we can go to the fancier one for dinner, since it won't get dark until after nine, we could still enjoy the views."

"Sounds like a plan, but let's start with the cellar and then after we do some exploring, we can decide about dinner. There is also an amazing Italian place with an outdoor seating area with great views of the town and the mountain. I've heard it's the place to go."

"I do love Italian. Let's do it."

Her heart swelled with pleasure as they entered the city with its Bavarian feel, even the Safeway and the gas stations had gingerbread trim and an abundance of flowers out front. Every single building had been fronted with the German decorations. Most had window boxes at both the street level and above, making it look like there were tiny balconies filled with flowers. There were hanging baskets on old fashioned streetlamps every few feet. In the summer there were horse drawn carriages decked in flowers. Some buildings had murals painted on their fronts. It was such a cute town.

The cellar was just as he'd said it would be, packed, it was a couple of hours after the normal lunch hour but there was still a line down the stairs trying to get in and order. The smells wafting up the stairs made her mouth water and she wanted the other people to get out of her way. Fortunately, as they moved slowly, so very slowly, down the stairs some people were also going up the stairs, which she hoped would mean that they would be able to find a table when it was their turn.

They were finally seated at a tiny two-person table tucked in a corner, which was just fine with her. They ordered beer and brats, even though there were a number of other things on the menu that looked delicious. If they were eating there more than one time, she might like to try some of the other selections, but her mouth and heart were set on a path that was not going to change. Until she got her beer and brat there would be no trying other foods.

When she said as much to David he grinned. "I am right there with you, darlin'. Maybe if we come back for Christmas, we can spend a few days and try more of the offerings this place has."

"Except there are a ton of other places, we'd have to be here a month to try them all."

"Sounds good to me."

She just rolled her eyes at him because their food had arrived.

Their meal was delicious, David had ordered a sampler, so since he shared with her, she got to taste more than one variety of the sausages, but she was happy with her own selection of Bavarian Bratwurst with cold German potato salad and sauerkraut. They also tasted the different beers. David had picked a dark beer and she had picked a light one, again she was happy with her own selection although his was tasty, too.

∼

David was enjoying this trip to Leavenworth more than any other visit. Jacqueline dragged him into every single shop and he still loved it. The flowers in the hanging baskets, the people wandering the streets, the joyful sound coming from the stage, the smells from all the restaurants, merged together to create a cacophony of enthusiasm.

Even though she dragged him into every single shop, she only bought one thing, and surprisingly enough, that was a Christmas ornament, from the always Christmas store. Not him, he bought a giant bag of caramel corn, a variety of nuts, some cheese, two enormous pretzels, pastries, and fudge. He wasn't hungry in the least, but he knew he would want all of it when he got back to Seattle.

Jacqueline rolled her eyes at him. "You've bought enough food for a small army and there are still all those snacks in Betsy."

He shrugged as he paid for the pastries at the bakery. "But it's my only chance to buy things here."

"You can't possibly be hungry."

"No, I'm not, but when I get back to Seattle, I'll be happy I bought them. Even if I have to work out to keep my girlish figure."

She looked him up and down and raised her eyebrows. "Girlish? No. Sexy? Yes."

Warmth flooded him from her perusal, and he wanted to take her to their hotel, but check-in wasn't for another half hour. He had to keep wandering the streets before they could go there.

When they had been to every single shop, they wandered through the street fair, where there were lots of amazing artwork, but nothing to seriously tempt either one of their pocketbooks.

Coming out of the street fair, right by the pavilion, they stopped to listen to the performers. There were some dance clubs all decked out in their Bavarian costumes. So, they sat and watched the dancers.

David noticed many in the crowd had ice cream and they'd walked enough that he could squeeze some in. He piled his packages around Jacqueline and told her he'd be right back. He sprinted toward the ice cream shop and got them each a small cone—well as small as possible—which was still huge. But at least no two scoops for him.

He brought Jacqueline her waffle cone with butter pecan ice cream.

"David."

"Everyone else is eating ice cream, I didn't want to be left out."

She looked around and then back at him. "I didn't even notice, but you're right almost everyone has ice cream."

"It's a hot day. I brought your favorite."

"What if I wanted Rocky Road today?"

Oh shit, he should have asked. Before he could apologize, she laughed.

"Just kidding, this is my favorite."

Whew, dodged the bullet that time.

By the time they finished their ice cream, they were both ready to go to the hotel and check-in.

CHAPTER TWENTY-NINE

Lake Chelan

They checked in and put their belongings in their room, then decided a dip in the pool would be an excellent way to cool down. Even though Leavenworth was in the mountains it was still hot in the summer.

After splashing around in the pool with very little actual swimming, they were ready to relax before their dinner reservation, but first they took a long slow shower in the huge enclosure, that a family of four could fit in.

Nakedness and water, with a little soap, turned into much more than a simple cleansing, not that Jacqueline was complaining. But a small nap might be in order before they went out for dinner. Grateful for the hair dryer, she dried her heavy locks, and then she and David laid down for an hour. She was glad he'd made late reservations.

When they woke from their nap, they dressed for dinner and went to the restaurant, which had an amazing menu, and a wine list that couldn't be beat. Again, they sampled each other's food, and relaxed, enjoying the evening. No one seemed to be in a rush, so they dawdled long enough to order a dessert to share.

Jacqueline couldn't remember ever enjoying such a romantic evening. When they finally decided to leave, they held hands as they walked down the street. The night was still warm although cooling rapidly, as the colder air swept down from the mountains, and pushed the heat of the day away from the tiny town. The stars were bright, despite the lights from the surrounding buildings. The air so clean and pure it nearly hurt to breathe.

She knew she would remember this night for a long time. It would stand out to her as a once in a lifetime feeling of closeness with a very special man. She had trouble believing their relationship would last, once they got back to their real lives in the city. Jacqueline wanted it to continue, but she just wasn't sure she could pull it off. They would get busy and start making excuses. She'd never experienced anything different.

Then again, David was a different sort of man than the ones she'd dated previously, so if anyone could pull it off it would be him. She laid her head on his shoulder, he dropped her hand and put his arm around her to pull her in closer. She loved it, she hoped, wished, and even prayed a little, that they could find a way to stay together.

∼

David could almost feel Jacqueline turn pensive. He wondered what it was about. Their whole day had been amazing, and he knew she had been enjoying herself just as much as he had. So, what was this melancholy he could feel coming from her. She snuggled into his arms as he pulled her close, so he knew she wasn't upset with him.

He whispered in her ear, "What's wrong, sweetheart?"
She shrugged. "I just don't want this feeling to end."
"It doesn't have to darlin'."

A sigh whooshed out of her. "But when we get back to the city and start up all the work and responsibilities, how can it possibly stay this way? We'll both be running in opposite directions."

David knew, with them both being hard workers, that it would be difficult. Hell, they were probably both work-a-holics. But he was determined to find a solution. If he had his way, he'd ask her to marry him right there on the sidewalk in Leavenworth. But he knew she wasn't ready, and he also knew he had to come clean first.

He squeezed her tight. "We'll make it work. I'm not giving you up."

She put her head back on his shoulder. "I hope you're right."

He forced himself to walk slowly down the street, enjoying the romanticism of the evening. What he really wanted to do was claim her, fast and hard, no holding back. He was ready—more than ready—to make a commitment to her. He knew he couldn't, until he told her the truth about his job and his father, but he just couldn't reveal that yet. He wasn't secure enough in their relationship to know that she wouldn't bolt.

So, he craved to show her with his body. What he couldn't say out loud, he would demonstrate.

He whispered, "I want you."

She nodded. "I want you, too."

She didn't get it, something wild beat inside of him and it needed to come out. "No. I want to possess you. To brand you and make you mine, no holds barred. I want you under me, with me inside you, pounding hard and fast until you scream my name. And then I want to do it all over again, slowly and with infinite care, until we cannot stand it anymore and fling ourselves into the storm."

Jacqueline stopped and looked into his eyes for a long moment, and he worried that he'd gone too far. Had he scared her with his vehemence? Her eyes met his for a long time and he knew she could see the fire for her, burning in them, he couldn't hide it, he didn't want to hide it. He'd always treated her like a fine, fragile, honored woman. She still was that to him, but right now in this moment he needed more.

He waited patiently while she examined him. She gave him a wicked look. "Then why are we standing here in the street? Let's get back to the inn, and you can ravish me, and I will ravish you in turn."

They didn't wait another second, but by mutual consent they took off, nearly running down the street. They managed not to knock anyone down, but they got back to their room in record time. They charged inside, she slammed the door shut, and he flipped the night lock. She whirled him around and pushed his back to the door, her fingers clawing at his clothes.

He slammed his mouth down on hers and pulled the zipper down on her dress so fast he was afraid he might rip it. Her tongue dueled with his, and she pushed the sides of his shirt open, he heard one button ping on the floor.

"Oops, I missed one," she gasped as she drew in air.

He didn't give one damn about the shirt, he needed skin, now. David put a tiny bit of space between them and pulled her dress down to let it fall to the floor. She kicked out of her shoes and the dress, as she tore his shirt off his body and flung it across the room.

Her hands reached out for his chest; at the same time his hands cupped her breasts through the delightful scrap of lace covering them. He squeezed them and used the lace to abrade her tight nipples for a moment. But he wanted skin there too, so he unclasped her bra, she shrugged out of it, before plastering her chest against his, rubbing back and forth.

He grabbed her ass and hoisted her up, stepping away from the door so she could wrap her legs around his waist, her heat pouring over his stomach and cock. He walked her back to the bed and flung her on it, so he could tear the rest of his clothes off.

She wriggled out of her panties and had a condom torn open, before he could get out of his pants, shoes, and socks. Jacqueline took hold of his cock and got the protection on so fast her hands were a blur. Then she laid back on the bed, spread her legs and said, "Inside, now, hard and fast, David."

He could be obedient when he wished to, so he plunged into her, she gripped his hips with her legs, and his shoulders with her hands. They raced in heated passion, bodies slapping together, sweat dripping, mouths plundering, it was not pretty, but it was incredible. He nipped at her tits, with teeth and tongue, she cried out in ecstasy, so he did it again, and again.

Jacqueline's body tensed and he pounded into her harder and faster, until she came with an explosive cry. His name on her lips, he didn't let up and his motions drove her higher, until she sagged to the bed, he pumped in twice more and let himself go, with a shout of his own. Her name on his lips, his face buried in her hair, as he collapsed on top of her.

He needed to roll off of her, but he was spent, he had to take a few seconds before he could move. Even then, when he started to move, she held him tight.

"Just one more minute."

David gave her a moment and then rolled them both to their sides, Jacqueline left one leg over his hip. Her eyes were closed, and her lips were curved into an almost smile.

"I wasn't too rough, was I?"

She didn't open her eyes, but her smile got bigger. "Rough? Not at all. I loved every second of it."

She opened her eyes and the wicked look was back. "In fact, I think I should impose some sort of quota, one fast and wild per every three slow and easy. Or maybe two."

He laughed and squeezed her tight. She was his kind of woman.

CHAPTER THIRTY

Lake Chelan

David opened one eye to check the time, what he saw startled him enough to open both eyes and grab his phone. Dammit, he'd hoped the hotel clock was wrong, but it wasn't. They had less than thirty minutes until checkout.

He reached over to wake Jacqueline up and found nothing but cold sheets. Confused, he looked around the room, it was empty.

The door to the hall opened and she breezed in, bringing the delightful smells of coffee and food. "Oh good, you're awake."

"I'm not sure I would agree with you on that, why are you up and so chipper?"

"I had a great night last night and slept really well. Like the dead, you tuckered me out."

"Kind of my point, I'm exhausted."

The woman grinned back at him; it was such an unusual sight he wasn't sure he wasn't still dreaming. "Well you did do most of the work, so maybe that's why you're still lying about." She waggled her eyebrows at him, and he wanted to burst out in laughter. "We need to check out soon. Although when I went and got the breakfast, I asked them about checking out a little later and they were cool about it. Now come over here and get some breakfast, before it gets cold."

His stomach growled, so he got up in all his naked glory and stalked over to her.

She glanced down. "Well part of you seems to be wide awake."

He laughed; she was noticeably enjoying herself at his expense. And if they had more time, he would drag her back to bed with him. He was certain the hotel people didn't mean hours from now, so he pulled on his jeans, and filled a plate with all the different things she'd brought back for them to eat.

David could have eaten any number of the items he'd bought yesterday, but the breakfast smelled delicious. So, he dug in with gusto. She was no slouch in her breakfast eating either, they needed fuel after their night of passion.

He'd never felt anything similar, before last night, there had been an intensity to their love making, that had surprised him, which is probably why he was tired this morning, he'd stayed awake last night thinking about it. It had almost seemed like some kind of promise, and the intensity, he couldn't describe to himself, even after thinking about it last night, or rather this morning. He, who could wield words with the precision of a master, could not begin to describe how he'd felt last night. It was something that couldn't be defined by mere words.

He watched Jacqueline to see if she was feeling it too. He couldn't tell, she'd dropped off last night, like a stone sinking into a pool of water. He had worn her out, he could admit he felt pretty smug about that.

As he continued to watch, he noticed her movements were a little jerky, and she was a touch too chipper, no bubbly, that was the word, and in the fourteen days he'd known her, he'd never thought of her as bubbly. Was she nervous? He didn't want to be the only one that had noticed a change, but he didn't want her nervous about it either.

He swallowed. "So, about last night."

She jerked at his words, and coffee splashed onto the mini table, they were eating at. She grabbed a napkin and wiped it up, not looking at him.

"I don't know about you, but it felt different, somehow. I can't describe it, but there was something different. More intense, maybe." He shrugged, not knowing what else to say.

She sighed and dropped the wet napkins on her empty plate. Her eyes met his, through her lashes. "You felt it, too?"

"Oh, yeah. It kept me awake last night, trying to figure out what had happened, what had changed."

"Those same questions greeted me this morning, when I got up to pee. I couldn't get back to sleep and lay there with my thoughts churning."

"So, I'm a night worrier, and you're a morning one. Good to know. We'll take shifts."

A smile flitted across her lips. But her eyes were still looking fearful, no not fearful exactly, cautious maybe. He pulled her close. "Don't be worried, we're bound to feel different as our relationship progresses and changes. I've never gotten this far into a relationship before, so it's bound to be new."

She sighed and snuggled in closer. "Okay, just as long as I'm not the only one feeling it."

"Nope you've got no corner on the market, sweetheart. I'm right there with you. We can be uncertain together." She relaxed into him and he felt like they'd turned a corner. What corner, he didn't know, but he was willing to continue on the path of discovery.

Jacqueline wasn't exactly sure what had just happened, but she felt better. This *real* relationship thing was much harder than she had guessed it would be. It was much more awesome at the same time, so she supposed it was worth it. Couldn't she just have the good part and ignore the scary part? Not how the world worked, but it would, if she had her way, which she didn't.

She packed up all their purchases and clothes while David showered. They needed to get moving, if only for the checkout period. She wasn't all that excited about getting back to Seattle and dropping David off. Her empty house held no appeal. Maybe they could find things to do on the way back. At least that would postpone the inevitable split.

David came out of the shower all damp and sexy, and she wanted to pull his clothes back off and drag him to the bed. She managed to restrain herself, but just barely.

It didn't take them long to get on the road heading for home. She managed to keep her tone light as they talked about things they liked to do in Seattle, and things they'd never done before. She couldn't help wondering if David was making a list in his head, about possible future outings.

When they got near Steven's Pass he asked, "Would you like to stop and maybe ride the ski lift? I've always wondered about doing it."

She lept at that idea, it would give them more time together. "That sounds like fun, we can stretch our legs, too."

David looked incredibly pleased with himself and she wondered if he was feeling dread at them separating, as much as she was. They spent two hours at Steven's pass, riding the chair lift up, and walking back down on the scenic trail, then they played disc golf, like a couple of kids.

When they got back in Betsy, they were ready to continue down the mountains.

They'd had a good breakfast, but when David suggested stopping in Monroe, for a hamburger at a pub he knew about, she was all for it. The exercise on the mountain had given her an appetite, and she knew her house was devoid of food. Deliberately. She'd given all her fresh food to a neighbor, knowing it wouldn't last the two weeks she'd be gone. There were still meals in the freezer, but stopping with David in a pub sounded a lot tastier and infinitely more fun.

She ordered a barbeque bacon burger and he ordered a huge monstrosity of a thing, with a double patty of hamburger, a chicken breast, and a load of bacon. How he could possibly eat all that food she didn't know. They also ordered a flight of beer to taste. It was all locally brewed.

They took their time eating and tasting the different beers. Somehow David did manage to eat his enormous burger, she didn't know where he put it, did he have a hollow leg?

"I can't believe you ate that whole thing. I don't even know how you could bite into it, but you did manage it."

"It was delicious, too."

She shook her head at him. "I gathered that, since there is not a scrap of it left. How you can eat like that is astonishing."

"It's all your fault."

"My fault, how do you figure?"

He leaned in closer and gave her a hot look. "You use up all my energy and I have to refuel."

She gulped and felt her cheeks flame. "Oh."

He took her hand and brought it to his lips, and an inferno roared through her.

She tried to pull her hand back, but he didn't let go, and continued to drive her wild with desire.

"David, stop. Not fair, we're out in public."

He looked up and around the room. "I don't see anyone I know. Do you?"

She managed to extricate her hand and looked around. "No, but that's not the point."

He sighed and sat back in his seat. "All right, I'll behave... for now."

"Good." She took the last of the beer she favored and gulped it down, trying to cool the inferno he'd built in her. It didn't help much.

David took his favorite and finished it. "I'm about ready to go, if you are."

She was ready, she needed fresh air and sunlight, to try to vanquish the heat inside her. It was late afternoon, and she decided they had dawdled long enough. There were a couple of things she needed to do before morning.

Apparently, David had decided the same thing, because he directed her to his house and gave her a warm kiss, but nothing incendiary. "Next time you can come in and I'll barbeque something. I'll call you. Have a good night, sweetheart." Then he gathered all his purchases and suitcase, and waved goodbye from his porch.

She drove off to her own house, a little sad that he hadn't invited her in. But then she thought about all she needed to do before tomorrow and shook off the feeling.

She got home to her house that she loved, and wheeled her suitcase in. A second trip and she managed to get all her purchases in, except for the picture, which came in on the third trip. She dropped all her purchases on the dining room table, and propped the picture still in its wrapping against the couch.

Her house felt large and empty, and so quiet, but she was determined not to think like that, and rolled her suitcase into the laundry room, where she could start the first load. She was dropping the clothes into the washer when a piece of paper drifted out. She picked it up and saw it was a note from David, on it was a heart and just some simple words. 'See you soon my love. David'.

Her heart melted and she wanted him here with her. Or she could go there. Darn it all, she knew what she wanted, but also knew what she needed, and that was some time to get her life together, for tomorrow. She had to meet with the lawyer in the afternoon. That thought managed to dash her lovesick attitude to the floor.

She didn't find any more love notes hidden in her clothes. But she wanted to call him in the worst way. She finally went and plugged her phone into the charger to keep her from calling. Just as she plugged it in a text message dinged. It was from David.

David: I miss you.

Jacqueline: I miss you too.

David: My house is so empty. I wish I'd invited you in.

Jacqueline: I feel the same, but I do need to get ready for tomorrow.

David: Me too.

Jacqueline: Adulting sucks.

David: LOL it does. Have a good night.

Jacqueline: You, too.

Jacqueline laid her phone down with a sigh. She felt better—no less lonely—but just knowing he felt the same relaxed her. She put away her purchases and unwrapped her picture.

She wanted to hang it in her bedroom where she could think of David and the fun they had had on the lake. When she'd bought it, she'd been torn between there and the living room, now she was certain she wanted it in her bedroom. The picture already had the wire on the back to hang it. All she needed was a nail or a picture hanging bracket.

She went to the kitchen to look through the tool drawer, which was really a junk drawer, but she liked to call it a tool drawer and make it sound more important. She was elated when she found exactly what she needed.

Twenty minutes later the picture was hung and level. Not every woman had a level in her tools, but she did, and it made her infinitely happy to do a good job. She sat back on her bed and smiled at her picture while she waited for her clothes to dry.

CHAPTER THIRTY-ONE

Lake Chelan

David walked into the law firm, both determined and nervous. He had never really confronted his father, and he wasn't sure how much the other partners were like his dad. It might be a futile attempt at making a change. If it was, and all the partners were like his dad, then he knew he would have to change companies. He couldn't in good conscience stay with the firm.

Even if they were interested in what he had to say, and wanted to find a better way, he wasn't sure he wanted to keep working with his dad. He'd realized being away for the two weeks, that his father made small cutting remarks every time he saw him, which made David question himself and poked tiny holes in his self-esteem. It wasn't healthy.

The company always had a meeting on Monday mornings where issues were brought up and discussed, so that meant he didn't have to call a special meeting. When it got to be his turn to bring up issues, he could just mention what he'd found out in Chedwick, he didn't even have to mention Jaqueline's name, and everyone would assume he'd heard about it from Sandy.

He had a few minutes to check messages left by his legal aide, he'd already gone through his email to remove the rubbish and flag the ones he had an action item for. He'd prepared notes on what he wanted to talk about with the other lawyers, and had gathered information on what it would have cost Jacqueline's company in man-power, physical costs, and an idea of what the delay had done to what should have been their holiday sales, and the difference it made in having to delay until the spring. Since their game wasn't out at Christmas, people had selected something else. Some of them would have still bought it in the spring, but not as many as the holiday sales would have been.

He was as ready as he could be, so he pulled the briefs out that he'd made, picked up the notebook he used for these meetings and his coffee and walked to the conference room. It had an old-fashioned conference table that spoke of wisdom and wealth, the chairs around the table were plush swivel chairs, the most expensive available. Part of the extravagance was to impress clients and part of it was to make the lawyers feel important.

His aide, Diane, was already in the room so he greeted her. They had a meeting planned for later, to discuss the issues that had arisen while he was on vacation and any office info he needed to know.

They normally did a round robin during this meeting, with each person bringing up the issues that were on their plate and if there were any concerns. David deliberately picked the spot that would make him last up, because he was fairly certain it was not going to be a quick and easy conversation.

His father walked in and sneered at him. "Back from Hicksville I see, and about time too. Why you needed to take two weeks is beyond me."

David wasn't about to get into it with his father now, he

had much bigger issues to fight about, planned for later in the meeting.

Franklin Jade had followed his father into the room. "I found Chedwick very restful, and the people warm and knowledgeable, when I was there. David probably has at least another month of vacation he hasn't used."

He had five weeks, but was staying out of this discussion.

Henry snorted. "That was a fool's errand of yours, also. Stupid woman was probably asking for it.'

Franklin's jaw tightened but he didn't respond, he'd had the same attitude about spousal abuse, until his daughter had been murdered by her husband.

David's father must have realized his gaffe because he muttered, "Not that some men don't take it too far." He waved his hand in a vague manner and took his seat, keeping his mouth shut, which David found quite refreshing.

The discussion around the table was not terribly interesting. His father didn't even mention the sentencing for the game company, clearly, he had moved on. He was not going to be a happy camper when David revealed all he knew.

When it got to David's turn, he opened the file folder to the report he had made. He was going to start talking and hand around the info when asked for it. "You all know I was in Chedwick last week. While I was there, I found out more information on the sabotage case that Henry was working on." His father insisted on him calling him by his name while they were in meetings.

Henry spoke up, "That case is done. We got the conviction. Only the sentencing is left."

David nodded. "Yes, and that's good, but I believe we need to take a more proactive stance at the sentencing. The company lost a lot of money from that sabotage and I believe we need to get some of that recompensed to them. It would help cover their losses and also send a message to other companies, that corporate espionage and sabotage are not going to be swept under the carpet."

His father scoffed. "I knew you going back to spend two weeks in that place would make you a wimp. You always did have a thing for Sandy."

"Sandy is happily married to Greg Jones, and she has nothing to do with this discussion. This is a matter of right and wrong."

Henry's face darkened with anger. "Right and wrong have nothing to do with it. If the other company had retained us first, we would have worked just as hard to get them off. As it was the information was sketchy. It's a white-collar crime, hardly worth our notice." His father grinned. "But they did pay well, for a nice long time."

David was getting pissed, but he wasn't going to let it show. "It wasn't a white-collar crime, those people put pornography in a children's game. If it had gone out it could have had devastating consequences."

Henry waived his hand in a vague manner. "A few tits and some ass, the kids these days see more than that on TV."

"Did you request proof of that, Henry? Do you know what porn was placed in the game?"

"No, but…"

"Well I did." He handed the stack of printouts to his aide who passed them around the table. "The first page is what it cost for the Tsilly game to be cleansed of the porn, shown at the top, and at the bottom the lost earnings estimates of missing the holiday release. The next few pages have a few examples of what kind of pornography was placed in the game. The last page is my proposal for our actions moving forward."

David sat back and watched as the attorneys and aides around the table flipped through his document. He saw raised eyebrows at the dollar amount it had cost them to rid the game of the porn. It was a significant amount.

The next few pages caused faces to drain of color and a green tinge settled on some of his colleagues. The porn was not as his father had said, a few titties and ass, but it was graphic and pushing the boundaries. He knew some people indulged in the things shown on the pages, but it was definitely not what people would want their children to see, even if they themselves chose to participate.

His father's two partners looked at Henry and raised an eyebrow. Henry raised his hands in surrender. "I didn't know."

Jeremiah Klout stared at Henry for a moment. Then he said softly, "Maybe you should have checked into it a little more, rather than being all pissy about having to work with women."

Jeremiah didn't wait to hear what Henry had to say, he simply turned to the last page and began reading the proposal David had lined out.

His father turned his embarrassment about not doing a good job into anger and glared at David for a few moments, before also turning to the last page of the document. David watched as his father stiffened further, as he read down the last page.

When he was done, he huffed out, "That is a ridiculous plan, I won't do it. It will make Williams, Jade and Klout look like a bunch of fools. Like we didn't do our homework and went into the trial blind.

Since that's pretty much the way he felt about what his father had done, David didn't argue. In fact, he wasn't even looking at his dad, he was watching the other two partners.

Franklin sighed and set the document on the table. He pulled off his glasses and pinched the bridge of his nose. David had only seen the man do that a few times, but when he had, it portrayed that he was uncomfortable and trying to make a hard decision.

Jeremiah tossed the paper onto the table and looked at Henry then at Franklin. Franklin nodded and shrugged. A breath whooshed out of Jeremiah; David had never seen him so discombobulated. "Whether you want to do it or not, Henry. It needs to be done."

Henry grimaced. "I think we should make David do it. It's his hotshot idea after all."

Franklin and Jeremiah exchanged another glance. Franklin said, "I think that would be an excellent idea."

His father startled at the words, then he bristled, finally he relaxed. "Excellent. I have a meeting set up with the game company for this afternoon, at three. If we're finished, I need to go work on my next case." Without waiting to see what anyone said, his father stood and marched out of the room, ceremoniously dropping David's report in the trash.

David's aide scurried over and pulled it out of the trash. "This needs to be shredded." Everyone left in the room nodded and passed their copies toward Diane.

∼

Jacqueline was not looking forward to the three o'clock meeting. She'd gotten to the office early and had gone through emails. As the team came in, several of them stopped by her office, to ask about her vacation, and to let her know they were glad she was back.

She had a team meeting scheduled for late morning with a catered lunch, and the cookies she'd brought back from Samantha's bakery. So, they could work through any issues that had arisen while she was gone. Sandy would Skype in, Jacqueline was the business lead of the team, not the technical lead, that was Sandy's job. But since Sandy was now living in Chedwick, Jacqueline had begun sitting in on the team meeting, on the off chance they needed any management support.

She usually didn't do much more than listen, but she did get a flow for how they all worked as a team, and it had prompted her to discuss promotions with Sandy, while she was in Chedwick. Sandy agreed with Jacqueline's assessment, so in a few days Jacqueline would be able to announce some changes. She didn't think anyone was going to be sad about the promotions.

They had a relaxed meeting but got a lot accomplished. When Sandy hung up, the team loitered, munching on cookies, and waiting to hear about her vacation and what she thought of Sandy's town. They had all been there before, for Sandy's wedding, and before that, for the amusement park grand opening, but none of them had stayed longer than a weekend, so they were eager to hear about all her adventures.

They finally left the conference room at two, she was glad there hadn't been anyone else scheduled in the room and they could take their time. Jacqueline had felt her phone vibrate a couple of times, but had not pulled it out of her jacket pocket. She didn't allow phone usage during meetings for her team, or herself.

As she walked toward her office, she scrolled through the calls. All the calls had been from David. There were also a couple of text messages asking if she could have lunch with him, or if he could stop by her office any time before three. He seemed a little frantic, but she really didn't have time today. She only had a few minutes before the meeting with the legal firm, and she needed to gather her notes, and make sure she still looked professional.

She'd worn a pretty, turquoise halter dress with a long black jacket that kept her curves from being too obvious.

Normally she didn't worry about such things, but Henry Williams was an ass, who didn't like women, so she tried to downplay her femininity when she was going to be meeting with him. She probably shouldn't have worn the turquoise, but it made her happy to look at it. It reminded her of the bright blue skies in Chedwick, so she'd decided to hell with some man and what he thought, and had worn it.

Second thoughts were trying to make themselves known, but it was too late to change, so she would just roll with it. She checked her hair and her makeup, touched up her lipstick, smoothed her dress and buttoned the jacket. That was as good as it was going to get. She grabbed the spiral notebook, and walked out of her office, locking it behind her, sad that they'd had to implement that rule about locking office doors.

She hoped someday they would be able to go back to the casual office style they had had before the sabotage. The saboteurs had caused a lot more damage than just the porn in the game. Her heels made a rapid tap-tap-tap as she moved toward the executive conference room. She wasn't a bit sad she'd missed what should have been the sentencing date, but it did cause her to feel a little out of the loop.

She was the first person in the conference room, so she debated where she wanted to sit. She finally decided to sit with her back to the windows so she could see everyone's face, none of them would be in silhouette that way. She also selected to sit towards one end of the table rather than in the middle, since she didn't want to be too close to the jackass lawyer. Who always marched in and took the center chair.

Several other people from her company came in the door, all of them leaving the center chair open and sitting along the window side of the room. The company heads that had taken Henry Williams to dinner would sit on either side of him, sometimes he brought an aide, who sat behind him like some sort of minion. Most of the time he came alone.

Everyone was in place, but Mr. Williams was still not there. Jacqueline wondered what had happened, they had set up arrangements for him to be cleared through security ahead of time, and he'd been to this room on multiple occasions. Had the jerk stood them up? It would be just like him to do so.

Finally, the door opened and one of the admins stepped into the room and stopped dead. "So sorry everyone, there was a mix-up at the check-in desk, but we've got it all sorted out now."

Then she turned and hurried away, leaving Mr. Williams to catch the door and make his way into the assembly.

Jacqueline stopped breathing when David walked into the room. What was he doing here? How did he get in? She didn't have time to talk to him now, couldn't he see that. She'd told him she would be in a three o'clock meeting.

David smiled at everyone, his eyes lingering on hers in what looked like trepidation. Then he looked back to the room at large and said, "Hello, I am David Williams, and I will be handling the rest of your case, in lieu of my father."

What? Handling the case? His father? What in the holy hell was he talking about? Everyone went around the table introducing themselves, and she managed to spit out her name and job title at the appropriate time, but her thoughts were spinning.

She didn't hear a whole lot of what was said over the next hour, and what she did hear made almost no sense to her frazzled brain, but her co-workers and the upper executives were beaming with excitement when the meeting concluded. They had never looked thrilled at the conclusion of any of the other meetings, so whatever David had said, they were very happy about.

Everyone gathered around him shaking his hand and slapping him on the back. They were talking animatedly and grinning from ear to ear. Jacqueline got up and walked out the door, while he was still swarmed with her co-workers. She had no intention of making nice. She was totally pissed at him, even if he *was* going to make things better.

CHAPTER THIRTY-TWO

Lake Chelan

David saw Jacqueline leave the room, while he was surrounded with her associates. He wanted to chase after her but was stuck. The executives offered to buy him dinner and a drink, and while he probably should make nice and go with them, he had to find Jacqueline to explain. He'd glanced at her several times, during his explanation about what he wanted to go for during the sentencing, and she'd looked confused.

He didn't think she'd heard two words. Even during the question and answer period, she just stared straight ahead. He had almost seen her mind whirling with a completely different set of questions. Then when he was finished and everyone stood to shake hands, she'd marched out the door. Everyone else in the room had big smiles, not Jacqueline, she was furious. He didn't blame her one bit.

He'd tried to get ahold of her to explain but she'd not answered his calls or texts. So, she was totally unprepared for his arrival. Dammit, how could everything spiral out of control in less than a day? But it had.

He had to find her and beg her to forgive him. But he had

no idea how to do that, he couldn't just wander around knocking on doors until he found her, it was a big building. The executives were standing by, to see if he would go with them for dinner and drinks.

He hated to ask, but it was his only choice. "I was wondering if you could direct me to Jacqueline Hurst's office. I need to speak with her for a moment."

One of the execs, Bradford he thought, said, "Absolutely, have you met her before?"

"Yes, in Chelan, last week."

"So, does meeting her have anything to do with you taking over the case for your father?" Tyrone, the other exec, asked.

"She did mention what went on, and since I've known Sandy for years when I explained what I wanted to do she gave me a couple of samples of the porn to show my firm."

Tyrone shuddered. "Nasty stuff for kids to see."

David agreed, "Yeah, even before I saw what it was, I knew more needed to be done than what my father had planned. Even simple naked pictures would have warranted it, but what they put in there was criminal. I've sent those pictures to the judge, by the way."

They had arrived at Jacqueline's office, so he knocked on the door. There was no answer.

Bradford shook his head. "She never leaves her office door shut when she's in there." He knocked on her door and called out her name. When there was no answer, he took keys out of his pocket and opened the door. The lights were off, she was clearly gone for the day.

Tyrone's eyebrows shot up. "Jacqueline never leaves this early."

Dammit, David was screwed, he had to find her immediately if he was going to have a chance in hell of making her understand. "Would you guys mind if I take a rain check on dinner and drinks. I need to see if I can catch Jacqueline."

Bradford gave him a look. "Mind explaining?"

He didn't want to get into it with anyone except Jacqueline, but he realized he didn't have her address, so if he was going to find her, he would need their help.

"Maybe in one of your offices?"

"Sure, mine is right down the hall," Tyrone said.

When they were settled into his office with a helpful shot of whisky, David said, "I didn't tell her I was an attorney, after dealing with dear old dad she was pretty anti-lawyer."

Both men stiffened and he held up a hand. "She had every right to feel like that. My father can be very cutting towards women or anyone else he feels is not equal to his exalted self. I've known him all my life and the guy can be an ass. He's good in his profession and knows how to spin a story, but personality-wise he ruffles feathers, and doesn't care."

David shrugged and soldiered on. "Anyway. I didn't tell her any of that, so when I walked in today, she wasn't ready for it. I'm sure she feels like I lied and betrayed her, and in a way, I did do that, but not to hurt her. Just the opposite in fact…"

His mind flashed back to every moment of the last two weeks, her laughing in the sun, her face-planting in the water, her under him flushed with pleasure. Image after image assailed him.

One of the men cleared his throat which brought David screeching back to the present. His face heated, and he stuttered out, "So, I need to find her and explain, as soon as possible."

Bradford gave him a fatherly look and Tyrone still looked skeptical.

"I promise I won't do anything, if you would just give me the street she lives on, I'm sure I can find her house."

"The street? Not the address?" Tyrone asked.

"Yes. I know you can't give me her address. I could have the information dug up by a colleague or two of mine, but... I already know to start looking in Issaquah, and I feel certain I can find her house if I can narrow it down to a single street. She has very unique tastes."

Bradford laughed. "That she does." He looked at Tyrone. "What do you think?"

"Fine, if he can find her house with just the street name, I suppose he knows her well enough to deserve a chance."

Bradford told him the street and then added. "If things work out, we'll all go to dinner and for drinks, maybe after the sentencing."

David nodded with a confidence he didn't feel. He had no idea how he was going to convince her he wasn't a lying ass. Shit.

∽

Jacqueline just sat in her chair on the deck, completely stupefied. She had no idea how she'd even gotten home. She'd charged out of the building in a rush so David wouldn't be able to catch her. She'd known she had only a couple of minutes before he would come to find her.

She didn't want to talk to him. The liar.

He'd lied to her for two solid weeks. The first lie had been bad enough, but this second one was a doozy and she had no intention of letting him off the hook.

Her mind whirled as fact and fiction intertwined. Images from the past two weeks collided with him walking into her conference room in his suit. He'd looked amazing in his black suit with a black shirt and a power red tie.

How could he be so deceptive? They'd had so much fun. He'd been the first man she'd really ever connected with, but that man was a myth apparently. What else had he lied about? She couldn't trust him about anything.

She couldn't even function at this point, she'd dropped her purse and jacket inside the front door and brought out a glass of ice water to the deck to think. So, she sat on her pretty patio with all the flowers and tried to make sense of it all. Going from angry, to sad, to hurt and betrayed, then back to angry, in a continuing cycle.

She heard her sliding door open and looked up to find David walking out of it. That act finally knocked her out of her haze and she realized that she was boiling mad. She stood and marched over to him, grabbed him by his tie and shook a finger in his face. "You are a lawyer."

"Yes."

"I hate lawyers."

He shook his head and spoke softly. "No, you hate my father, there's a difference."

She narrowed her eyes at him. "I don't believe you."

"Not all lawyers are evil. Some of us want to help."

She supposed that might be true. But it didn't change the facts. "You lied to me."

His brow furrowed. "No. You never asked my last name or what I did. I simply didn't bring it up."

That made her want to growl. "So, lies of omission."

"If you must, but if you'd just met the woman or man of your dreams and they hated what you did, and in fact hated your father, would you have brought it up?"

She frowned. "No, I suppose not, but it still feels wrong."

"I'm sorry. I tried to get ahold of you before the meeting to explain, but you never answered."

Oh, now it was her fault? Yes, he had called and left multiple messages, but he'd had two weeks to tell her. He hadn't needed to surprise her like he'd done. "I was in a meeting. Besides, we've been together for two weeks, you had plenty of time, before walking in here today."

"Actually, I didn't. When we had our Monday morning meeting, I pointed out what exactly had gone on with your company, and my belief that the saboteurs needed both jail time and to pay restitution, my father took himself off your case and told me to handle it. So, I've only known a couple of hours."

"The whole time I was in my meeting."

"Ah, so you weren't just ignoring me?"

"No. I don't allow phone calls or texts during meetings, so I have to abide by that rule also, we finished maybe a half hour before the next one started. What do you mean restitution?"

"You didn't listen to my presentation?"

"No. I couldn't think I was too shocked you walked in, and then you were the lawyer we were meeting with. I couldn't process it, or the betrayal I felt."

"I'm so sorry about that. A short recap, your company lost a lot of money from the porn, in man hours cleaning it out, in all the media that had been created but had to be scrapped, and in sales lost at the holiday season. So, we are going to press for jail time for the extremely harmful porn they put in the game, and then we're going to sue their pants off. I've already sent a small sample to the judge of the porn you cleaned out."

She frowned. "How did you get that?"

"Sandy."

"Of course." Sandy had kept some of the images in case they needed them for the trial. No one else had wanted them left around, they felt they were too dangerous.

Bringing herself back to the present she said. "Well I'm still not happy with you for lying to me, but I did manage to notice how happy everyone was when I left the room."

David looked at her beseechingly. "Are you going to forgive me?"

She folded her arms across her chest, she wasn't giving in to his puppy dog look. "No. How did you get into my house?"

"You left the front door open."

Well hell. Not a big surprise, since she didn't remember getting home, let alone shutting the front door. "How did you find it to begin with?"

He shrugged. "I got the street name from Bradford and Tyrone."

She nearly screeched. "They gave you my address?"

"No, just the street name."

That didn't make sense, the street was a couple of miles long, how would he know which house was hers? "But it's a long street, how did you know which house?"

"Because I know you."

"Seriously?"

"I knew it was yours the minute I spotted it, but I forced myself to drive down the whole street, just to make sure."

She wasn't buying it. "But that's impossible."

"Not when someone knows you like I do. I knew what to look for. Besides, I could feel you here, I know it doesn't make sense. But when the love of my life is only a few yards away… I just knew."

She'd felt a magnetism toward him before, so she supposed that might be true. "Love of your life, huh?"

"Yes, do you forgive me?"

Tsilly whispered in her thoughts, 'Don't let anger rule over your heart'. So, this is what those words had meant. She shook her finger at him. "Are you going to stop lying to me? What else did you lie about?"

The puppy dog expression came back. "Nothing, I swear. Only what I was terrified to tell you."

"But."

He pulled her close. "No, buts. I was a goner the first moment I saw you, leaning over that counter telling Sandy about all the fun you were going to have reading novels. Then you spun around and that was it, I knew I had to make you mine. And I would have lied, cheated, and stolen for the chance. So not introducing myself as David Williams, lawyer from Seattle, was easy."

She grimaced. "If you had introduced yourself that way, I would have driven off to find a place in one of the other hotels for the two weeks."

"See there, so I even saved Carol from both of us leaving, because I would have followed you and she would have lost all that revenue. "Do you forgive me? I promise to never lie again... except maybe about Christmas presents. Please forgive me, and let me make it up to you, every day for the rest of your life. I love you, Jacqueline."

She wanted to cry. "Oh, David, I think I love you too, which is why it hurt so bad."

He kissed her forehead and then looked in her eyes. "Never again, baby. I will never lie to you again."

Jacqueline couldn't deny reading the truth in his eyes. She wanted to be with him enough to trust him again. Tsilly had told her to let go of the anger, to trust her heart and the peacock had seconded it. "And you're going to roast that other company?"

"Oh yeah, you can count on that."

"Okay, I will forgive you. But..."

"But, what?"

"Your father. I'm not sure I can be civil. He's an ass. I cannot imagine sitting across the table from him for Christmas dinner."

"You probably won't need to worry about that. After I stood up to him today, he may never speak to me again.

Besides, I may not stay with his company, which is really going to piss him off."

"Really? Why don't you want to stay there?"

"I want to help people." He shrugged. "I don't want to be constrained by the rules of that firm. They don't take many pro-bono cases. I want to take on whoever I feel like representing, not who pays the best. If that other game company had gone to the firm first, my father would have worked just as hard to discredit your company. I don't want to be like that."

Her eyes shone with approval and that's all he needed to see. He pulled her into his arms and squeezed her, then his mouth descended, and she could feel his relief pour through the kiss. He really had been scared she wouldn't forgive him. As her senses started whirling again, for a much different reason, she vowed to remind him of this moment, if he ever pulled something like that again.

That was her last thought as they went on a sensual journey of which only lovers could know.

EPILOGUE

Lake Chelan

Jacqueline sighed; she was disappointed they wouldn't be taking the snow train to Leavenworth for their Christmas celebration. They were still going to Leavenworth, to see the Christmas lights and enjoy the festival, just not on the snow train. They needed a car.

After they spent the weekend in Leavenworth enjoying the Christmas celebration, the first weekend of December, they would be travelling to Chedwick, to spend Christmas with David's mother.

They would be staying in the bridal suite at Carol's B&B, because between the weekend in Leavenworth, and Christmas, they would be getting married.

Yes, he'd managed to convince her to be his wife.

She sighed and looked at the flash of diamonds on her finger. Her ring was gorgeous with a big center diamond and smaller accents of rubies. He knew exactly what she would love and had picked it out.

When he'd finally convinced her to marry him, he'd run

out to his car and come back in with the ring. He'd even gotten down on one knee to propose.

He'd knelt before her with the ring box in his hand, "Jacqueline, my own sweet love, my goddess, my own personal Aphrodite, I love you more than mere words can say. Will you make me the happiest man on Earth? Will you marry me and walk beside me for the rest of our days on this planet?"

She'd already told him yes.

But apparently, he wanted to make things official, silly man, he'd already stolen her heart. "Yes, David, I will marry you, I love you and look forward to many years to come."

Then he'd pulled the ring out of the box and slipped it on her finger. She'd gasped at how perfectly it fit both her finger and her personality. That's when the waterworks had started. He knew her. David knew her better than any other person had ever known her, except maybe her father.

She knew her dad was looking down on them and smiling.

They'd decided not to wait, but to turn their planned December trip to Leavenworth into a month-long adventure. Starting in Leavenworth and eventually ending there. With Christmas and their wedding in Chedwick.

When they'd called to book reservations in Carol's Bed and Breakfast, she'd laughed and told them she'd kept the bridal suite open for them.

She sighed again at the memory.

David asked, "Why the sighs?"

"Just thinking about all that's happened in such a short time."

He grinned, "Yeah, only five months and I managed to snag you as my own. I was determined."

She reached across the console and poked him. "And persistent and nagging."

He took her hand and squeezed it. "I see it as persuasive and charming."

"You would."

"One thing dear old dad did manage to instill in me was not giving up. Probably not exactly what he'd had in mind, but it worked in my favor, so I'll take it."

"Yeah I guess I can't complain, it really has been a wonderful five months."

He'd surprised her with the other quilt she'd loved, when it had gotten cold enough to take the first one out of her blanket chest. The one Terry had made her. David had brought the second quilt over, the very night she'd put the first quilt on her bed.

"You bought me the other quilt?"

"I did, you loved it."

"But why now?"

"Because your blanket chest will be empty and sad about not being used."

She laughed and said, "David that's just silly. It's an object, it can't be sad."

"It certainly can. I'll show you." He'd grabbed her hand and dragged her to her bedroom, where her pretty quilt looked amazing on her bed.

He pointed to the blanket chest. "Look how sad and lonely it is."

She raised one eyebrow at him. He went and opened it and looked inside. "See it's lonely and needs a friend."

He carefully laid the new quilt inside it and made her look. "See, it's all happy, now."

It did look better inside with the quilt, but that was only because the comforter was gorgeous. She shook her head at him. "You are a silly man."

He looked inside one more time before carefully shutting

the lid. He pointed to the front with the pretty design Terry had carved. "Look I think it's smiling."

"Or maybe you're just crazy."

"Crazy for you. Absolutely."

Then they'd taken advantage of the very handy bed, after David had carefully removed the quilt.

Less happy thoughts intruded, David and his father. They still didn't know if he was going to attend the wedding. He'd never responded. David's father had not even acknowledged their engagement. David had called his father to tell him the news and had gotten a grunt in response. It was a short conversation. Better, she supposed, than Henry ranting and raving, about marrying her.

Of course, the fact that David had left his father's law firm, and gone on to take on the cases of people who needed help, and couldn't always afford it, probably didn't help matters. David did just fine for himself, though, because he'd done so well on the sentencing for the game sabotage, he'd made a name for himself in the corporate sector. So, the big corporations were the ones that paid the bills, and allowed him to work with the little guys.

What she found amusing was that when his name showed up for one of those little guys, as their counsel for a case involving a large corporation, those corporations immediately settled.

She was going to be the wife of a very good man. Even if his father didn't agree. It was Henry's loss.

~

David was over the moon excited. The day Jacqueline would become his wife had finally arrived. They'd had a fun time in Leavenworth during the Christmas lighting festival and had enjoyed seeing all their friends in Chedwick. But since arriving in town there had been a whirlwind of activity while they managed the last of the preparations for the wedding. They'd been going in opposite directions for days; he'd hardly seen her.

Both Jacqueline and he had been surprised by the number of people attending the wedding from the Seattle area, very nearly everyone from both offices had RSVP'd a yes. Fortunately, it hadn't been extremely snowy, so the roads were clear. The snowplows had managed to keep up.

What was very fortunate indeed was that the new building at the church was finished. Just barely, there was still some work to be done upstairs, and on the offices, but the sanctuary was finished. He was afraid, with everyone coming, that they were going to need the larger space. He took a quick peek out and sure enough the church was nearly full. People could squish together more if they had to, but it looked full to him.

Scott came up and asked, "You ready for this?"

"Hell, yes…. Oh, I suppose I shouldn't swear in church. Sorry."

Scott laughed, "The word hell has been heard a few times in the building, but if you want to feel bad about saying it, I won't stop you."

David grinned at the man he'd gone to school with. "You ready to marry me to my lovely bride?"

"I am, indeed, we worked like crazy to get the place done in time for your shindig, let's do it."

Scott led the way into the front of the church and David faced everyone he knew. His mom was up front and center, beaming at him. His friends from Seattle and this little town were all present. All except his father, he could admit feeling a little sad about that. He'd hoped his father would attend. Although if he did attend, he might act like an ass.

The music started and he drew in a deep breath, he

couldn't wait to see his beautiful bride walk down the aisle to him. There were a few people that would come before her, but he could be patient. She was worth the wait. Before the back doors were opened, he was shocked to see his father enter from the side area and slip into the front pew, next to his mother.

His mother beamed at his father and his father shrugged. Then he looked at David and winked. *His father had winked at him.* David didn't even know his father knew how to wink. If he hadn't been on display before the entire world, he would have... he would have... he had no idea what he would have done, because the experience was too surreal to anticipate. So, he gave his dad a smile and turned back toward where the doors opened.

He didn't pay a bit of attention to the other people coming down the aisle, all he had eyes for was Jacqueline. When she finally appeared in the door, he was frozen.

Greg, whom he'd asked to be his best man whispered, "Don't lock your knees. You don't want to pass out."

That got him to relax and he focused on his goddess, all dressed in white, with red accents, she looked amazing. The ceremony was a blur, but he knew he had spoken his vows with a loud clear voice. It was the best part in his opinion, pledging himself to Jacqueline.

When Scott said he could kiss his bride, he gave her a sweet, closed mouth kiss, that was perfectly appropriate for church. She'd frowned at him, grabbed him by his lapels, and hauled him in for a kiss that sizzled, and in no way was appropriate for church.

Scott had laughed and the rest of the guests did too. So, David had nothing to complain about. The reception was being held in Amber's banquet hall, which gave them time for a few more kisses, as Greg and Sandy drove them to the second location.

David barely noticed the new hall. He supposed some people would gush on and on about how great it had turned out, but David's entire focus was on Jacqueline.

They ate, they danced, they cut the cake. At one point his mother had sidled up to him.

"Something's wrong with your father," she said in a hushed voice.

David looked around but didn't see his dad. "What's wrong?"

"He's being nice."

David chuckled; his dad was capable of being pleasant when it suited him. "Mom—"

"No, he's being nice to everyone. Me, Sandy, Greg. It's kind of scary. It's like he's a different man."

"You're exaggerating."

"No really, it's like he's found religion or something. I can't explain it."

"I suppose I can go talk to him and see for myself."

David saw his dad enter from the hall near the restrooms, he was smiling and talking to the man who was the janitor at the school. David was certain his father had never spoken to the man in his life, so he decided he should go see what was up. Jacqueline was talking with Mary Ann, so it was a good time. He nudged her and said, "I'll be right back."

He strode across the room and right up to his dad. He held out his hand. "Henry, I'm glad you could make it. We weren't sure you were coming."

His father looked embarrassed for a moment, and then grabbed David's hand and pulled him in for a bear hug. "Sorry about that. I didn't know until the last moment myself."

David was shocked, first the man had used the S-word, he had *never* heard his father utter that word. Ever. And his father had hugged him, and not a fake superficial hug but a real bone breaking type of hug.

"Dad, what's up? Are you dying or something? You're not acting like yourself."

His father laughed. Out. Loud. A big deep belly laugh. "I suppose I deserve that. No, I'm not dying. I just, well… Let's sit down for a moment. Jacqueline won't mind, will she?"

"No, she's talking to Mary Ann."

When they were settled at an empty table. Henry said, "The day you defied me about how I had handled the game case I was furious. So furious I was ready to write you out of my will."

David didn't care a flip about his father's will, so just waited for him to continue.

"No, you wouldn't give a damn about that would you? Anyway, then I got to thinking about the case and the way I handled it. I thought about that disgusting porn and realized I'd done a piss poor job on the case. Yes, I won it, but only because I knew how to spin it to the judge. The more I thought about it, the more shame I felt, knowing that I'd failed as an attorney."

David didn't know what to say, so he continued to hold his tongue.

"When you went after that other company and did such an outstanding job, I was so damn proud of you. But I was a coward, and didn't call to congratulate you, because I was still mired in remorse, over my own actions."

David could never remember his father ever saying he was proud of him. His heart swelled with joy, but he knew there was more to come. He muttered, "Thanks."

"Then you left the firm and that felt like a slap in the face. My own son leaving the company I had worked so hard to build. I was crushed, not that I would let on I felt that way, I just acted angry. It was better to be pissed than crushed."

"Dad, it wasn't about that."

"I know. My therapist finally pointed that out to me. You are cut from a different cloth. You always did want to help people and I wasn't the slightest bit interested in that. I was making money to prove to the world that I was successful."

David's head was whirling. A therapist? Prove he was successful? Who was this man and what had he done with his father?

"Dad, I'm feeling kind of confused here."

"Of course, you are. But I see Jacqueline looking this way. I'm sure she's worried I'm being my previously normal ass-ish self. Just, well, just know I've changed, and I want to have a relationship with my son and his very beautiful and intelligent wife. I promise not to be a misogynistic ass."

David's thoughts were whirling, what in the hell was going on, was this some kind of joke? He searched his father's eyes for deception or humor and found none. His father was being perfectly honest.

His dad looked over his shoulder. "Here she comes now, to save you from my clutches."

Henry Williams smiled so big David thought his face might crack. "Jacqueline you look lovely. I'm so glad you came to join us. But first, I must beg your forgiveness for treating you, and your sabotage case, with disdain. It was not well done of me and I have been feeling the sting of remorse, ever since David shone the light on the truth, which I did not bother to look for. Can you find it in your heart to allow us to start over? I would like very much for a second chance to prove to you I have changed my views on nearly everything."

David was certain that Jacqueline was now reeling in confusion. He stood and wrapped his arm around her waist to steady her.

She looked at him wide eyed and then turned to his father. "Is this some kind of joke?"

His father shook his head. "No, it's not, but I know it must be hard to believe. Let me prove it to you over time. Maybe we can meet for drinks after your honeymoon. We might work up to dinner."

Jacqueline frowned. "We can meet for drinks and see how it goes."

"Excellent. Now may I say, welcome to the family. Thank you for not letting the sins of the father, rest on the son. He's a much better man than I."

Jacqueline opened her mouth, but no sound came out.

His father smiled and waved them off to return to their wedding party. "Enjoy your party and I'll see you both in January."

As they walked away Jacqueline whispered. "He looks like your father. What the hell happened?"

"I have no idea." He shrugged. "Let's do the bouquet throwing thing and get out of here."

"That's exactly why I was looking for you. I'm so ready."

"Excellent, where is our photographer? We have to have pictures, or it didn't happen."

Jacqueline laughed, but didn't argue. "Let's ask Sandy, she's the one who recommended her, when *our* photographer ended up with a broken leg, from that stupid shot she was trying to get for that other couple. I can't imagine asking a photographer to climb up on a roof for a bird's eye view. What is wrong with people?"

Just before they got to Sandy, they saw the photographer, Deborah, and Terry, march into the room, glare at each other and go in opposite directions. David wondered what that was about, but he didn't care enough to ask. He wanted to take his beautiful bride back to the bridal suite, and spend the next week locked inside it, making love to her. They could come out for Christmas eve.

The End

ALSO BY SHIRLEY PENICK

LAKE CHELAN SERIES
First Responders
The Rancher's Lady: A Lake Chelan novella
Hank and Ellen's story
Sawdust and Satin: Lake Chelan #1
Chris and Barbara's story
Designs on Her: Lake Chelan #2
Nolan and Kristen's story
Smokin': Lake Chelan #3
Jeremy and Amber's story
Fire on the Mountain: Lake Chelan #4
Trey and Mary Ann's story
The Fire Chief's Desire: Lake Chelan #5
Greg and Sandy's story
Mysterious Ways: Lake Chelan #6
Scott and Nicole's story
Conflict of Interest: Lake Chelan #7
David and Jacqueline's story
Another Chance for Love: Lake Chelan #8
Max and Carol's story
Frames: Lake Chelan #9
Terry and Deborah's story
Christmas in Lake Chelan: Lake Chelan #10
Ted and Tammy's story

BURLAP AND BARBED WIRE SERIES

Colorado Cowboys

A Cowboy for Alyssa: Burlap and Barbed Wire #1

Beau and Alyssa's story

Taming Adam: Burlap and Barbed Wire #2

Adam and Rachel's story

Tempting Chase: Burlap and Barbed Wire #3

Chase and Katie's story

Roping Cade: Burlap and Barbed Wire #4

Cade and Summer's story

Trusting Drew: Burlap and Barbed Wire #5

Drew and Lily's story

Emma's Rodeo Cowboy: Burlap and Barbed Wire #6

Emma and Zach's story

SADDLES AND SECRETS SERIES

Wyoming Wranglers

The Lawman: Saddles and Secrets #1

Maggie Ann and John's story

The Watcher: Saddles and Secrets #2

Christina and Rob's story

The Rescuer: Saddles and Secrets #3

Milly and Tim's story

The Vacation: Saddles and Secrets Short Story

Andrea and Carl Ray's story

(Part of the Getting Wild in Deadwood anthology)

STAND ALONE

Helluva Engineer - Patricia and Steve's story

ABOUT THE AUTHOR

What does a geeky math nerd know about writing romance?

That's a darn good question. As a former techy I've done everything from computer programming to international trainer. Prior to college I had lots of different jobs and activities that were so diverse, I was an anomaly.

None of that qualifies me for writing novels. But I have some darn good stories to tell and a lot of imagination.

I have lived in Colorado, Hawaii and currently reside in Washington. Going from two states with 340 days of sun to a state with 340 days of clouds, I had to do something to perk me up. And that's when I started this new adventure called author. Joining the Romance Writers of America and two local chapters, helped me learn the craft quickly and was a ton of fun.

My family consists of two grown children, their spouses, two adorable grand-daughters, and one grand dog. My favorite activity is playing with my granddaughters!

When the girls can't play with their amazing grandmother, my interests are reading and writing, yay! I started reading at a young age with the Nancy Drew mysteries and have continued to be an avid reader my whole life. My favorite reading material is romance, but occasionally if other stories creep into my to-be-read pile, I don't kick them out.

Some of the strange jobs I have held are a carnation grower's worker, a trap club puller, a pizza hut waitress, a software engineer, an international trainer, and a business program manager. I took welding, drafting and upholstery in high school, a long time ago, when girls didn't take those classes, so I have an eclectic bunch of knowledge and experience.

And for something really unusual… I once had a raccoon as a pet.

Join with me as I tell my stories, weaving real tidbits from my life in with imaginary ones. You'll have to guess which is which. It will be a hoot!

Contact me: www.shirleypenick.com

To sign up for Shirley's Monthly Newsletter, sign up on my website or send email to shirleypenick@outlook.com, subject newsletter.

Follow me:

- facebook.com/ShirleyPenickAuthorFans
- twitter.com/shirley_penick
- instagram.com/shirleypenickauthor
- goodreads.com/shirleypenick
- bookbub.com/authors/shirley-penick

Printed in Great Britain
by Amazon